FOREIGNERS
BARBARA
SAPERGIA

All stories © Barbara Sapergia, 1984 and 1989.

All rights reserved. No part of this book covered by the copyrights hereon may be reproduced or used in any form or by any means—graphic, electronic or mechanical—without the prior written permission of the publisher. Any request for photocopying, recording, taping or information storage and retrieval systems of any part of this book shall be directed in writing to the Canadian Reprography Collective, 379 Adelaide Street West, Suite M1, Toronto, Ontario M5V 1S5.

In slightly different form, two chapters of *Foreigners* were published in *Canadian Ethnic Studies* and another chapter was broadcast on CBC Saskatchewan's "Ambience" radio series.

These stories are works of fiction. Names, characters, places and incidents either are the product of the author's imagination or are used fictitiously. Any resemblance to actual persons, living or dead, is coincidental.

Cover and inside design by Carolyn Deby.
Cover drawing by Denis Nokony.
Typeset by First Impressions Ltd.
Printed and bound in Canada by Hignell Printing Ltd.

Barbara Sapergia thanks the Saskatchewan Arts Board and the Canada Council whose assistance provided time to work on the manuscript of *Foreigners*. Thanks as well to David Carpenter, Robert Kroetsch, Jack Hodgins, and the writers of Prairie Factor for encouragement and many helpful suggestions.

The publisher gratefully acknowledges the financial assistance of the Saskatchewan Arts Board, the Canada Council and the Department of Communications.

Canadian Cataloguing in Publication Data

Sapergia, Barbara, 1943 -
      Foreigners

ISBN 0-919926-35-5

I. Title.
PS8587.A64F6 1984   C813'.54   C84-091337-0
PR9199.3.S364F6 1984

Coteau Books
#401 – 2206 Dewdney Avenue
Regina, Saskatchewan
Canada S4R 1H3

To all the Sapergias

November 1912

Chapter
ONE

Stefan stared and stared. He knew he should do something. Trian lay white and still. Blood had spilled from his mouth, soaking the white sheet. It couldn't be true, the doctors had just been here. Yet he saw Trian, wrapped like a long white package, on the floor by the bed.

Sofie touched Trian's forehead, said it was still warm. She expected him to do something. He didn't want to think about it, but he knew there was nothing. If the boy's throat had filled with blood, he could not be breathing. The blood would have choked him.

Stefan moved to the chest of drawers, picked up a cracked hand mirror. Kneeling beside Trian, he held it to the boy's mouth, then examined it for any sign that breath still moved in him. There was none. Sofie watched in disbelief, her face stretched tight, only a nervous tug at the corner of her mouth threatening to shatter the mask. Stefan got out and looked out the window.

It was almost dark now, heavy snow falling, wind gathering force. A storm was coming, the doctors had just outrun it.

Luba and Nicu stood in the doorway, afraid to speak. They wanted Stefan to talk to them, tell them everything was all right. They wanted to see him smile, watched his face longingly. Sofie moaned, running her fingers through Trian's dark hair, and along his cheek. Hearing, Stefan felt pain in his throat, fierce and tearing, the way it felt when you ran on cold winter days. Outside, snow was falling, thicker and thicker, driven by wind against the naked frame house. He saw himself out on the snowy road, running, running to catch the doctors.

Stefan turned to Nicu and Luba. He had to think to make his arms and legs move. He put an arm around each of them and led them from the room. He took them downstairs to the living room and made them sit in chairs around the table. "Trian is dead," he told them. Although Luba and Nicu were almost grown up, their faces were now the faces of children. Children who have seen something they can never understand. Luba began to cry, first softly, then in choking sobs. Nicu cried soundlessly, his chest heaving. Stefan felt the tears strike his own eyes, and hot pain seemed to swallow his throat, his stomach. He could not cry now. He patted the children's shoulders, stroked their hair. "I must go to mama now," he told them.

Stefan lit a coal oil lamp and went back up the dark stairs, the glowing light moving with him, enclosing him. In the cold room, Sofie still sat on the floor, Trian's head on her lap, her eyes black and burning. Trian's dark blood had trickled down the side of his face and wet her dress. Stefan bent and touched her cheek, icy against his fingers. He put the lamp on the dresser, got a blanket from the bed. Very gently, he wrapped it around Sofie's shoulders.

When he tried to lift Trian's head from her lap, she turned fiercely towards him, as if she would prevent him, but still she made no sound. Stefan lifted the child's head, settled him carefully to the floor. Sofie stared at him as he lifted her body, rigid but unresisting, and got her to her feet. He hoisted her in his arms, somehow folding the stiff limbs so he could hold her, and carried her to their bed. He set her down still wrapped in the blanket, smoothing out the bent legs. He brought more blankets and tucked them around her, then held her, his body partly covering hers, trying to warm her. Downstairs the children were crying, but Sofie seemed not to hear. She still didn't cry, only looked at him without seeing, and he had to turn his face away from that look. After he'd held her for a long time, he looked again at her face and saw that she had fallen into a kind of sleep, her body still held tight.

Slowly he lifted his body away from hers, careful not to jar the bed, but she never stirred. He took the lamp and went downstairs.

Luba and Nicu were asleep sitting up on the sofa. Stefan carried Luba to her room, hardly aware of her weight, put her into her bed still dressed, only stopping to take off her shoes. From the boys' bed he brought blankets to cover Nicu on the sofa, not looking at the small figure still wrapped in the sheet. After he'd covered Nicu with blankets, Stefan sat down at the round table. He rested his head on his folded arms and tried to think, but the sound of the howling wind filled his mind. He got up to put more coal in the pot-bellied stove. When he held the lamp to the window, he saw only whirling snow in the shallow space where the lamplight spilled out into the darkness, and his brain felt tired as he tried to focus on the dancing flakes. Cold drafts whipped through the room, sucking away his body's heat. Fine powdered snow drifted in through cracks around the doors and windows.

"It's his tonsils," the young doctor had said, the one with the blonde hair. "We'll have to take them out."

Stefan knew he should follow them and kill them. He kept seeing them as they left the house, too much in a hurry to stay and eat, but so quiet and polite. He saw himself helping them with their coats, beautiful warm coats of heavy dark cloth, with thick fur collars, fur-lined gloves of soft leather. He realized now that something had been wrong with the young doctor's clothing. His cuffs had no longer shown, starched and white, beneath the sleeves of his suit jacket. He'd seen it, even then, but it had meant nothing.

"Is there any medicine for him?" Sofie had asked when the doctors had finally come down from Trian's room.

"No," the old grey one had said, "he won't be needing any medicine."

He kept seeing these fine English doctors fastening their coats, opening the door, saying goodbye. That was the time when he could have stopped them. He remembered something else. There'd been no mention of payment.

Stefan wanted to follow the smoothly gliding cutter, to follow them and kill them. He wanted to cut their throats, make them bleed as Trian had bled. There was a sharp knife in the kitchen, the one they used to cut meat. He wanted to see the doctors' fine warm coats soaked in their blood, staining the close-woven grey cloth, clinging in drops to the fur collars, staining dark the smooth satin linings as their bodies grew cold. He wanted to see the pale polite faces when the knowledge of death was in their eyes.

He wanted to kill these men, as he'd sometimes wanted to kill the boyar in his old village. He'd come all this way to be free of the boyar, and of the desire to kill anyone. And now it seemed that nothing had changed.

Near dawn, Stefan climbed slowly up the stairs. He carried a basin of warm water, soap, and a towel. In the boys' room, he laid Trian on the bed to wash him. As he looked at the face, it seemed as if the child was about to speak to him, and Stefan couldn't stop himself from touching the lips. But they were cold, as he had known they must be. He had never handled a dead person before, but he knew that at death the bowels and bladder empty. Very tenderly he washed his son, the smooth cold skin, and found him clothes in the dresser. As he worked, tears fell down his face, but could not ease the burning core of pain in his throat and chest. Trian's eyes were still open, a beautiful dark brown that no longer had expression. Stefan closed them. He dressed the boy in a blue wool shirt and dark serge overalls that Sofie had made. He found clean socks and Trian's small boots. He sat on a chair by the bed and looked at the boy. Trian would have been four years old tomorrow.

Stefan remembered Trian's birth, during their first winter in Canada, before the dry years and parched crops had driven them off their homestead to rented land. That first year their garden had been good, and Sofie had filled the cellar with sauerkraut and canned vegetables. Winter had come early, and by the middle of November the land had been covered by three feet of snow. On a clear cold night, Sofie gave birth to Trian, their first child in the new country.

He remembered the murmuring voices in the night, entering his dreams, and Sofie crying out, and then the thin wail he was hardly sure he heard. He remembered sitting up in bed, seeing pale light through the curtain that separated their bed from the kitchen, where Luba slept; hearing Nicu's even breathing in the loft above, and then the soft wailing began again. And Sofie, lying back in Luba's bed, her unbraided hair falling in waves to her shoulders, the baby lying quietly on her belly. "He wasn't like the others," she told him. "He was such an easy baby, I didn't want to wake you."

For a moment, remembering, Stefan believed nothing had happened. His mind felt lighter, freer. Then the memory faded, although his tired mind fought to hold it, leaving a sick feeling of guilt. In the lamplight he saw again the cold pale face.

Stefan collected the soiled sheets from the bed and took them downstairs to the kitchen. He put them to soak in a boiler half-filled with cold water melted from snow. His arms and legs felt as weary as if he had run after the doctors in the cold snow. He put more coal on the stove. When he opened the door to the porch off the kitchen, chill wind driving through the cracks cut into his body, and he thought too late of his sheepskin coat. By the light spilling into the darkness from the lamp in his hand, he quickly found what he needed—some pieces of old lumber, a can of nails, a saw.

Chapter
TWO

Stefan shook the reins, but Zaica kept the same slow pace, struggling to pull the sleigh across the drifted snow. After a night and day of bitter storm, the winter's first blizzard, the hills lay cold under a clear sky, deeper blue than he'd ever seen in summer. Today blue meant cold, in the sky and in the blue-grey shadows on the deep drifts across the road. Stefan had harnessed the horse after breakfast. By noon they would cover the eight miles to Coteau. He was going to see the doctors.

He'd thought of going to Chisholm for help, had looked across to the great stone house on the hill. Chisholm owned thirteen sections of this rocky hill country. They'd had to rent land from him after their homestead failed. After Stefan failed as a farmer. Now he was doing the same work he'd done in the old country. Raising sheep. He didn't mind, it was what he knew best. But Sofie had wanted them to have a farm. And neither of them had wanted to have a landlord ever again.

Stefan had stood watching the smoke rising from Chisholm's chimney, a white column breaking the solid blue of the sky. It was less than a mile away, but the trail through the coulees lay deep in snow. Watching the big house, the smoke, the deep drifted snow, he'd felt a surge of despair. He'd thought of Chisholm's stony face with its hard little eyes. Chisholm didn't know about their trouble and he wouldn't care if he did. Stefan had set out for Coteau.

He wore a sheepskin coat, had a blanket wrapped around that, but as the morning wore on, the chill crept beneath the warm clothes, to the bone, it seemed. He couldn't stop thinking about Trian in the small coffin he'd made. The day before, when the storm had finally ended, he'd worked with Nicu to dig a grave in the cold hard earth. They'd buried Trian as the sun set, Sofie and Luba watching from the kitchen window. Stefan kept seeing the small body, dressed only in shirt and overalls, nothing but the thin box to keep out the cold. He imagined the child lying frozen all winter, the body preserved whole and perfect until spring. Meanwhile, the sun shone on his own face, and he felt ashamed.

He'd tried to make a prayer for Trian before they filled in the hole. Sofie had wanted the priest, but he couldn't have that. It was hard for him to pray, but he made himself try. "Please,

Lord, take our child to a good place. He is a good boy." The words seemed bitter in his throat. He thought of the mother of Christ. "Maica Domnolui, please help Trian. He was good and kind, like the Christ child. Please help him now." He hoped it was enough. He knew there should be pomanas, food for the dead, so he put part of a sheaf of wheat in the coffin, and some brightly coloured ears of Indian corn. Nicu had cried as they filled in the hole, then outlined the mound in smooth white stones. Using smaller stones they'd outlined a cross at the head of the grave. Then Stefan had poured a glass of chokecherry wine over the grave, making a dark stain on the ground.

Now they were in sight of Coteau. Here in the last mile the hills flattened out into a wide plain around the town. To the west, less than a mile from town, stretched the range of hills that made up the Rowland family ranch. To the northwest, along the first ridge of hills, Stefan saw the raw gouges where clay was mined for the Rowland's brick plant, and it reminded him of graves. Today snow had blown into the pits, softening the harsh lines. The tiny figures of a few men moved slowly across the hillside, trying to dig a little more clay from the frozen ground before they would be laid off for the winter.

At last he reached the town. People had shovelled the snow away from their houses and stores, and a snow plough had been dragged down the streets, leaving huge drifts along the sides. Stefan stopped at the foot of the long main street, in front of the railroad station, to stare at a tall pine tree decorated with coloured balls for Christmas. Then he drove past Lazbee's store, where red and white striped candy canes and twisted red streamers hung in the window. All along the wide street, people walked briskly, glad to be out again after the storm. Stefan saw their gladness, but it was something apart, had nothing to do with him.

Stefan took the horse and sleigh to the livery stable and paid for oats and a warm stall. Zaica would have to take him all the way back home again that day; the long climb back into the hills was really too much for such an old horse. Stefan set off on foot down the main street, past the Rowland Hotel and the skating rink. Beside Meacham's Hardware Store was a small grey office building with the sign, "Wardham and Lawson, Barristers and Solicitors, Notaries Public," over the front door. There was another glass-fronted door at the side of the building, leading to a dark narrow staircase. Stefan went in this door.

He found it hard to climb the stairs. He wanted to turn and go home. What was he to say to these doctors? What was the use now? He thought of Sofie, at home, unable to cry; of

Trian, in the cold earth. He was ashamed of his fear.

Their names were printed on the door: "Dr. Owen M. Bentley" in large faded letters, and "Dr. James Markham" in smaller but newer letters. Stefan read very poorly, but he could make out the doctors' names. Beneath the names, a sign on the frosted glass said, "Please Walk In." He didn't want to. He forced himself to remember his boy.

Inside, two people waited to see the doctors: a young woman, obviously pregnant but pale and sickly looking, and an old man in farm overalls, too frail and bent to work anymore. They sat on worn leather chairs, the old man's cane resting against his chair. Behind a desk a woman sat, the doctors' nurse. She had thin lips pressed tightly together and little frown lines between her eyes. You had to talk to her if you wanted to see the doctors. Stefan walked to the desk.

"Excuse me, but I want to see doctor, please." It was the old one he wanted to see. "Dr. Bentley."

"Do you have an appointment?" the nurse asked, seeming to know he didn't.

"No, but I must see him." He tried to make his voice sound firm.

"And what is your name?"

"Stefan Dominescu."

The nurse looked at him hard. She rose from

her straight-backed chair, smoothing her long dark skirt. "Just a moment," she said. When she opened the door into Dr. Bentley's office, Stefan saw inside for a moment, saw there was no one in with him. The sight of the doctor set his heart racing. The nurse went in and closed the door behind her. In a few minutes she came out and nodded to Stefan. "Dr. Bentley will see you now," she told him.

Stefan got up, feeling the eyes of the other people on him. He felt very small and weak as he walked to the door, his hands moist, shaky. "Coward! Fool!" he said to himself, but it did not help. He opened the door and went in. The light came from electric lamps set in the ceiling, and it was very bright. The doctor sat behind a big wooden desk with panels in front that hid his legs. Around his neck was the thing for listening to people's hearts. On the desk were pen and paper, a leather case containing surgical instruments.

For a moment Stefan felt he must be making a mistake. It couldn't have happened as he remembered it. How could he accuse this man? Yet he remembered Trian, the cold lumps of earth falling on the wooden box. He looked at the old doctor's smooth polite face and felt the anger returning to him. He felt power coming into his hands, his arms.

"Yes, Mr. Dominescu," the doctor was saying,

"what can I do for you today?" His blue eyes looked very cold.

"My boy is dead." Stefan spoke very carefully so there could be no mistake.

"I'm very sorry to hear that," Dr. Bentley said. "He seemed all right when we left him the other day."

Stefan felt his mind cloud with rage. "He was not!" he cried. "Not all right! You kill him! You and the young doctor."

Dr. Bentley rose, keeping the desk between them. He spoke calmly still, but his voice formed a threat Stefan could not understand. "I assure you that Dr. Markham and I provided your son with the best possible treatment. The boy was perfectly well when we left him." He picked up a fine scalpel from his case and fingered it lightly.

"Liar." Stefan spoke in a low voice. "You leave him dead, wrap in a sheet. You leave him under the bed." His voice was getting louder, they would hear him in the waiting room. "Liar!" he yelled.

The doctor held his body stiffly, kept the big desk between them. "If you keep talking like that, I will see my lawyer about pressing charges. I don't have to listen to slander."

Charges? Slander? Could this doctor get *him* in trouble? He saw himself in prison, a dark and airless place, cold as the grave. Sofie and the children alone. But he couldn't give up now.

"I see the young doctor. He has no shirt on. Where is he? Let us ask him why he comes to my house wearing shirt, and leaves wearing no shirt."

"I don't know what you're talking about," the doctor said, but Stefan thought he looked worried. "In any case, Dr. Markham isn't here now. He's taking a short vacation over Christmas."

"He has gone away because he knows he did wrong," Stefan cried.

"Mr. Dominescu, surely you see that no one wanted any harm to come to your son."

"It's the young doctor. He doesn't know what he is doing."

"I tell you it's no one's fault!" the doctor said. "Do you understand?"

"You *know* he killed my boy!" Stefan insisted.

"He did nothing of the sort." The doctor's face twisted in annoyance. He looked at the big desk that stood between them. Stefan clenched his fists, and shifted his weight forward, as if he would throw himself at the doctor, even over the bulk of the desk.

"I assure you that if you were to take your boy's body to any other doctor, he would tell you that the treatment had been correct, and that the boy died from unforeseen complications." What did the doctor mean? Was he saying that other doctors would lie to protect him?

"I cannot bring him. He is already buried."

"Indeed?" said the doctor, and a smile touched his face. "And when was the boy buried?" It seemed to Stefan that the doctor grew larger as he talked. His body seemed to have no legs of its own, to be growing instead out of the massive desk.

"Yesterday," Stefan answered. "My older boy and me bury him."

"I see," the doctor said. "And where did you bury him?"

Stefan was confused. What did it matter where? "On our place," he answered. "On the hill behind house."

"Are you aware that it is an offence to bury a body on private land?" The doctor's fingers played with the scalpel. His hands were pink and clean, the fingernails rounded and smooth. He put the instrument back in its case.

Stefan's stomach felt sick. "What you mean?"

"I mean, Mr. Dominescu, that it is against the law to bury someone, as you have done." He savoured this triumph for a moment. "It is also against the law to bury a body for which no death certificate has been obtained."

Stefan felt unsteady on his feet. "What is death certificate?" he asked.

"A death certificate," the doctor spoke as if Stefan must be very stupid not to know, "is a paper signed by a doctor attesting to the cause of a person's death. Without such a paper, no one may be buried. To fail to obtain such a certificate is against the law, is a crime."

"A *crime?*"

"Yes," the doctor said, "a crime. Every person must have a birth certificate when they are born, and a death certificate when they die."

Stefan was confused. "Trian did not have this birth certificate paper."

"Indeed he must have had. Did not the attending physician prepare one?"

"Was no doctor there."

"In that case, Mr. Dominescu, I think you should be aware that it is also against the law to fail to register a birth. In the eyes of the law, it is as if your son never existed.

"It seems," he continued in a cold voice, "that you have broken a great many laws. And now you come here making slanderous accusations about my partner and me." His eyes were like sharp blue stones. "You must cease these slanderous statements. I will not let you destroy Dr. Markham's career. If you ever repeat these things to anyone else, I will be obligated to take action. I will see my lawyer and instruct him to press charges against you."

"But you kill my boy. You and the other one." The doctor's eyes were cold and blue, they seemed to float free from his face.

"You will only do yourself harm if you go on with this," the doctor said. "I tell you the treatment was correct."

"But you know he is dead when you leave our house. You *know!*" Stefan was getting too loud again. The nurse came to the door. The doctor nodded his head slightly and she went quickly away.

"I don't know any such thing." The doctor was no longer calm, no longer polite. "And I tell you, you can never prove it! No one is going to believe a man who has broken so many laws."

Stefan felt despair. If he told about Trian's death, the doctor said he would be charged. He didn't have the right papers for Trian, didn't even have the right to bury him. To prove what happened to Trian, they would have to dig up his body and have it examined by more doctors. He didn't want them to take Trian's body up again, handling him, burying him again. In town, in one of their cemeteries, far away from his family. And the doctors would all be friends of Bentley and the young doctor, would lie to protect them.

"You mean the law will not punish you?" he asked angrily.

"I am a respected member of this community," the doctor said. "And what are you? A sheepherder. A foreigner."

A black wave washed through Stefan's mind. The doctor denied doing wrong, yet he seemed to mock Stefan, saying he could prove nothing. He had left his village to escape the boyar, the cheating, the hatred. And nothing had changed.

"Then I punish you!" Stefan cried, moving towards the doctor's desk. The doctor shrank back against the wall. He looked towards the door, then at Stefan.

"Get back!" he cried. "Don't be a fool! You'll only get in worse trouble!"

The idea of worse trouble only made Stefan more desperate now. The doctor was looking at the door, balanced ready to run if Stefan came around the desk.

"I'm going to kill you," Stefan cried. "I'm going to kill you for what you do to my boy." He lunged across the desk, catching the doctor by surprise, and grabbed his throat. He felt a savage joy in his belly as he squeezed the skinny neck. He was going to squeeze the life out of this doctor.

Then arms seized him from behind, pulling him away, prying his fingers loose, bending them back until they almost snapped. Something struck him on the back of the head, and he fell to the floor. He couldn't move or see for the waves of pain in his head. He heard the doctor gasping for breath. He wanted to get up, but the floor seemed to pull him down, the cool dry wood dusty against his face, his hand. When he raised his head and looked up, he saw dark shapes against the light, two men looking down at him. If he tried to get up, would they hit him again?

Suddenly he understood; the nurse must have called the men. Very cautiously he raised himself to his knees. As his vision cleared he saw the doctor standing behind his desk, rubbing at bright red marks on his throat. Then the doctor spoke, his voice rasping.

"I want you out of my office now. And remember, I have two witnesses to this assault. They heard you threaten me." His chest heaved and he stopped to catch his breath. His eyes burned with anger and fear. "In case you were not aware, assault is a criminal offence. Or should I say, attempted murder?" He leaned over the desk, his voice cracking. "Now get out of here!"

Stefan started to get up, then stumbled back, dizzy and sick. The men were watching him, willing him to go. One of them took his arm and pulled him roughly up, pushing him towards the door. He walked.

Chapter
THREE

Stefan sat at the living room table, working on a flute, the careful strokes of his blade smoothing, caressing the clean reddish grain. Beside him, Nicu worked on a smaller flute of his own. Stefan followed his progress, now and then offering advice in a quiet voice. In the kitchen, water boiled softly as Sofie and Luba made cabbage rolls. All of them worked intently, seldom speaking. Today even the wind was quiet — a cold clear day, a day to take advantage of the afternoon sun to do close work.

Stefan watched as Nicu sighed and put down the little flute. Maybe the boy wondered when they would ever play these flutes. There had been no music in the house since Trian died. Everyone went about their work, but no one smiled. It seemed to Stefan that they were all lost in a feeling of heaviness, a dull pressure that weighed against the body.

The oven door creaked as Sofie put the

cabbage rolls in to cook, then the hinge snapped shut. He put his knife down, glanced at Sofie, then at the window. He thought he heard a tiny bell, far away. He heard it again, and glanced at Nicu who sat absolutely still, listening. Jumping up, they ran to the window, but couldn't see through the leafy patterns in the thick frost. In the kitchen, Sofie and Luba were also at a window. "Asha!" Sofie cried, barely louder than a whisper. Then they all raced for the kitchen door and out onto the hard-packed snow in front of the house.

A wooden sleigh drawn by a black team was gliding up the hill, a man and woman balanced neatly on the high front seat. The woman was tall and rather stout, but the man seemed huge, a bear of a man with his thick black hair and beard. Stefan heard the crisp slicing sound of runners on snow as the sleigh seemed to float up the hill towards him. Sleighbells rang clear and sharp in the motionless air. "Kosma! Nina!" Stefan cried, his breath making white clouds in the cold air. Nina raised her hand to wave, and he saw the colour in her cheeks, the red scarf at the collar of her dark coat. He realized he was holding his breath, his body tight and still, as he watched them approach.

Kosma reined in the shaggy-coated horses, their stamping feet stopping just in front of the porch. He jumped down, and so did Nina, not waiting to be helped, landing lightly in the snow. Now they all could move again, and Stefan saw Sofie throw herself in the woman's arms, crying, "Nina, Nina."

"Sofie, dragutsa," Nina answered, "we've come to spend Christmas with you." Sofie clung to Nina, tears running down her cheeks. "Sofie, draga, what's wrong?"

Stefan looked at the man, Kosma, and felt again the searing pain in his throat; tears stung, turned instantly cold against his eyes. Kosma looked at him, his calm grey eyes steady. Stefan clasped him, let his head rest a moment against Kosma's shoulder, the strong arms holding him. There was comfort in the sight of Kosma's shoulders and chest, enormous in his thick winter coat.

"Stefan?" he asked. Stefan just shook his head, couldn't talk yet.

Kosma turned to Luba and Nicu, gave each one a hug. Then he looked up at the sleigh where two figures were slowly emerging from under a heavy grey blanket: a boy, Paia, fourteen years old like Luba, and a girl, Petrica, just ten years old. Paia jumped quickly over the side, while Kosma lifted Petrica and set her down lightly in the snow beside Stefan, who kissed the two children in turn. "Buna ziua, Paia. Buna ziua, Petrica," Stefan said.

"Buna ziua, Uncle Stefan," they answered, although he was not really their uncle. He and Sofie were the children's godparents, and Kosma and Nina were godparents to Nicu and Luba.

Nina was leading everyone into the house, but Stefan stood a while longer in the cold air. Nicu came out again in his jacket to lead the horses to the barn. Sweat darkened their patterned red blankets as they trotted behind him, breath rising in clouds. Nicu, who loved horses, would take care of them.

In the kitchen, Sofie seemed distracted, trying to hang all the coats on one peg. The children, hovering near the stove to warm themselves, tried not to stare at her tear-streaked face. When Nicu came in from the barn, Stefan led them all into the living room. The adults sat around the oak table, the children on the sofa or floor.

"What has happened here?" Nina asked. "And where is little Trian?"

Stefan didn't know how to tell them. He was ashamed, he had been able to do nothing. As Kosma and Nina looked at him, he thought it would be easier to tell the story to a stranger than to them. But they must be told, so he took a deep breath, and began with the day when Trian had wakened with a bad sore throat. Sofie had wanted to send for an old baba in Kayville who knew how to heal people, but Stefan said no. In the old country they went to an old baba or the bonesetter, but in the new country they would have a doctor. He told how he had ridden to town for a doctor. How two doctors had come, one old, one young. He stopped to ease the burning in his throat. Finally, he told about walking up the stairs when the doctors were gone and finding Trian in the darkening room. Tears ran down Kosma and Nina's cheeks as Stefan spoke, but Sofie only stared in front of her.

"They just left? Said *nothing*?" Kosma asked.

"Nothing," Stefan answered, "just to let him sleep, and he would be all right."

"They said he would not be needing any medicine." The words were torn from Sofie.

"He was already dead when you found him?" Kosma asked.

"Yes," Stefan said, and Sofie looked at him sharply. "His face was still warm, but he was dead. The bleeding in his throat had stopped his breathing."

"Asha!" Nina said, as if she could not believe such things could happen.

"And now he is buried, and we had no priest!" Sofie said accusingly. "He wouldn't get the priest to baptize him, and he wouldn't get the priest to bury my boy." Her face stretched tighter. "Now what will happen to his soul?" Stefan touched her arm, but she pulled it sharply away.

"How could they do that? How could they kill my boy?" Sofie cried. "How could *he*"—she stared at Stefan — "let them do it?"

"Sofie — no!" he cried.

"You let them! You let them!"

"Sofie, draga, stop." Nina had her arms around Sofie, and now Sofie could hardly speak for weeping. "He let them," she moaned, "he let them kill my boy." The children looked at her in horror. These were the tears she had been keeping back, the thoughts. She couldn't stop now, clinging like a child to Nina.

A wave of new pain seemed to strike her. "I am sorry we came to this country!" she cried.

"You wanted to come too," he said, the pain burning again in his throat as if it would stop his breathing.

She shook her head furiously. "You talked about it day and night till I agreed. I could see you would give me no peace. And now my boy is dead!" Then Sofie seemed to collapse against Nina as, at long last, she cried her grief for Trian. Nina led her upstairs to the bedroom, but Stefan still heard her weeping, harsh and painful.

There was something more he had to tell. "He said we don't have the right papers," Stefan said. "There was a paper we were supposed to get when Trian was born."

"A birth certificate," Kosma said. "You must go to town and register a child when it is born."

"The doctor said it was like Trian was never born," Stefan said. Kosma shook his head sadly.

"When the doctors left the house, the young one wasn't wearing a shirt under his jacket any more. I went to town to accuse them, and I remembered about the shirt. Kosma, it seemed like the old doctor looked scared when I told about the shirt."

"The young one isn't there any more," Kosma said. "Nina took Petrica to the doctor, and that nurse said he was gone for good."

"That is proof then," Stefan said. "He ran away."

"Maybe you could go to the police," Kosma said. "Maybe they could find him."

"He could be far away by now," Stefan said. "And I don't want them to take up Trian's body from the grave. What good would it do now?" His mind came back to the idea that haunted him all the time now. "If only I told them no."

"Stefan," said Kosma, "you could never have known that." He put his arm around Stefan's shoulders, held him tightly. "You could never have known." The children still sat quietly.

"Petrica," Kosma said gently, "would you help Luba make some coffee for everyone?" The girls got up and moved to the kitchen. "Nicu and Paia, will you help me carry some things I have in the sleigh?" The boys went to help Kosma with parcels and large pots wrapped in dishcloths. One, a big cast iron pot, he put in the oven to heat. Then he sent the boys to the barn, to see if the horses needed anything, or if elves had taken the harness. Then he brought his own big coat and Stefan's sheepskin, put on his coat and helped Stefan into his. They could still hear the weeping, Nina's voice soft and comforting, as they went out into the porch.

Stefan let Kosma guide him up the hill. The icy air brought cold tears to his eyes. Kosma pointed southwest, towards the sun. On either side, it was flanked by coloured lights, like fractured pieces of the rainbow. They seemed to dance before his eyes, to cast their glowing light on the snow.

Stefan stared at the snow as though he'd never seen it before. It only seems white, he thought. It has as many colours as the sky. Filled with tiny ice crystals, the air seemed to hum around them, the golden-violet fire of the sundogs bending and scattering across the snow. The colours seemed to be everywhere, he and Kosma covered in light.

Watching the pulsing sky, touched by that cold and distant fire, Stefan felt his body answer to the cold. It seemed to him that winter was the real season in this country, the warmth and growth of spring and summer only a pleasant dream hovering over the hills.

Stefan gazed over the snowy hills, ridge on ridge blending to a smooth sweep along the horizon. His body ached to fill those spaces, to be part of that long curving line. When he'd first

come to this country, he'd thought of it as open
and free. But now he knew that already it was
owned, and some men owned far more than
others. Like Chisholm, his landlord, snug in his
big stone house. And to the northwest, beyond
the elevators of Coteau, the high ridges of the
Rowland ranch. Twenty sections owned by one
family.

And yet he wasn't sorry he'd come. The
rhythm of the hills held and satisfied his eye.
There were other people trying as he was to make
a better life than in the old country. Kosma and
Nina in their place at Spring Valley. People in the
farmhouses to the north, marooned in the un-
tracked snow, pillars of smoke rising straight
above them, dissolving in a sky that was cloud-
less, yet hazy with ice crystals. As far as he could
see, nothing moved, only the silent hovering col-
umns of smoke. The air seemed to throb with the
music of the spinning ice, and he thought he
could hear the piercing screams of sundogs.

He looked down at their own house, its naked
boards worn almost to a shine in the glancing
light. There they endured — visiting no one, cooking their meals, feeding and watering the sheep
that sheltered in the shed on these cold days,
sleeping away the long night, only Sofie really
busy, cooking, cleaning, spinning, knitting. Only
Sofie hard and bitter, refusing to cry out her grief
or speak her bitterness. He felt pity for them and

for the people on the scattered farms, held fast in their frail shelters, living on reserves of food and warmth harvested from the brief summer.

He thought of Luba and Nicu, moving through the days, held in a slow dance with the waning sun. Did they long as he did just to drive to Coteau, to see faces they had never seen, other people and buildings, horses and sleighs? They never complained, just waited, carrying out their few chores. Every night before bed, they played crokinole on a cracked board abandoned by the Chisholm children, played it each day as if it were a new game. All the while waiting, as he waited, for Sofie to cry or speak. Now she had cried, spoken.

In the last fiery light from the dying sun, it was impossible not to feel touched. He still missed the child every day, thought of him almost every moment, and yet he felt that the light touched him. Kosma was right, he could never have known. All his life he would be sorry, but he didn't have to hate himself any more.

Kosma was looking at him, quiet grey eyes fastened on his face. He didn't need to speak, just to be there. They turned. Again Kosma put his hand on Stefan's shoulder. They walked down the hill, the air icy, painful in their lungs.

In the house the girls had set the table and put out bread and butter, pickles and sour cream. The boys had put more coal in the stove and lit the coal oil lamp. Already it was almost dark outside. The weeping had stopped. Luba and Petrica brought in the big pot of cabbage rolls, each carrying one end, and set it in the middle of the table. Everything was ready. The children looked to Stefan and Kosma. Nina came slowly down the stairs. Sofie was not with her.

"I think we should go ahead and eat," she said.

They all gathered around the table. Stefan hung the lamp on a hook over the table. Nina went back to the kitchen and rummaged in the packages they'd brought. In a moment she was back with glasses on a tray and a bottle of chokecherry wine. She poured a glass for each person, even Petrica. Kosma said a blessing.

Stefan sipped the wine, the warm taste of chokecherries that have grown sweeter after the first frost. He took bread and cabbage rolls, with butter and sour cream and pickles. Stefan found he was very hungry, and he thought the food had never tasted so good. Again, he felt an easing in his heart, a lightening. These were good people, his own people. He raised his glass: "Buna sanatate, my dear friends," and they replied, "Buna sanatate." The room was bathed in warmth from the food, the wine, and the warm glow of light.

When the plates were finally cleared away the girls brought coffee and Nina went to her packages again and brought another surprise. From a small bottle she poured a little into each glass. Stefan sipped—ah, the warmth of tsuica, plum brandy, and he was back in the village. The sweet plums of old man Radu, his pears and raspberries. For a moment he thought only of summer, birds singing, the ache of tangy fruit against his greedy mouth.

On the wall, Stefan's violin hung from a wooden peg. Kosma lifted it down and used his handkerchief to wipe away the dust that had gathered on it. He lifted it and began to play, a song from the old country. It was a sad song, the notes pulled and drawn out in a slow agony that could not be hurried or avoided. The violin seemed to be tuned to their bodies, as if the sounds vibrated within them. It is like the heart speaking, Stefan thought, as it told him that life is a sad thing, full of wickedness, that can never go well. It told him the many different ways that life could come round to sadness, almost more than you could bear. Then the music grew gentle as it told him of beautiful things now lost. Stefan felt the ache in his chest and throat again, saw his little boy as a baby playing with sticks and pebbles in the dusty yard of the homestead, looking up at him with a smile. For some reason this simple picture came to him again and again. The music said he was gone, would never come again, not on this earth. The music said he must accept that, and the tears flowed down his cheeks, the children crying too. He looked at Kosma, holding the violin as delicately as a mother holds a child, tears in the kindly grey eyes. Then he heard a sound and turned to see Sofie sitting on the stairs, tears streaming down her face. Nina rose and led her to a chair a little apart from the others.

No one spoke when Kosma finished the song. Then he began to play again, a lighter, softer song. The song was still sad, but it seemed to tell of the coming of spring, when the earth would be alive and warm again. Stefan knew this song, had always loved it. He and Kosma had learned it as boys. It always reminded him of new lambs playing on a spring hillside in the meadows of Ramoiesti. He saw grass and flowers, felt soft breezes blowing through his hair. With trembling hands, he picked up his flute. He joined Kosma in the song, his flute singing high above the melody like light-footed goats on the mountain that climb away from their shepherd. The flute and the violin sang two separate songs, and together they made a new song never heard before. Kosma played the song the way they learned it as children, but Stefan played a new melody that came from inside. He would never play it in the old way again. The song seemed about to stop, then again and again it found a new path, with now the flute leading, now the violin. Suddenly, there was nothing left to play, and they stopped on the same note. For a moment no one moved or spoke. Then Kosma hung the violin back on its peg. He took the flute from Stefan's hands and placed it on the table.

Then Sofie and Luba were bringing straw ticks and bedding, making Kosma and Nina a warm bed on the floor. One by one, people slipped outside to the outdoor toilet, then without being told, the children disappeared up the dark stairs to bed. Petrica would sleep with Luba, Paia with Nicu. Sofie smoothed the plump chicken-feather pillows for Kosma and Nina.

"Good-night, dear friends. Sleep well."

"Good-night, Sofie," they answered. She walked up the stairs.

"Good-night," Stefan said, and slowly followed, leaving Kosma and Nina to put out the lamp.

Stefan's legs felt terribly tired as he climbed the stairs. He felt they had lived through the day of Trian's death again, and the tiredness pulled at his arms and legs. At the door to the bedroom, he hesitated. He could see Sofie lying in bed, her face and shoulders framed in moonlight from the window. He undressed slowly and folded his clothes neatly over a chair, then lifted the covers and climbed into bed beside her. For a long time they lay side by side, not moving, hardly breathing. Then it seemed that she moved, turned a little towards him, and he thought he could feel the warmth of her. He turned a little himself, saw her eyes watching him in the dark, and he reached out to her. She moved into his arms, pressing her warm head against his shoulder.

He wanted her so much, had needed her for so long. She must know it wasn't only pleasure he wanted, but the comfort and love of her body. His mind seemed to ignite with tiny explosions as he entered the warmth of her. That was what he needed, to touch her there, feel the energy that was in her. She wanted it too, she moved with him, and their bodies relaxed, little by little, with soft shudderings. She was crying softly, couldn't seem to stop, but it was so comforting, so good, he didn't want to hurry, his coming seemed to go on and on, seemed to bring hers, like soft waves pulsing around him.

For a long time afterwards they lay awake in the dark, their eyes wide open, looking into the pale moonlight. Then without any feeling of drowsiness, they were asleep.

May 1913

Chapter
FOUR

He moved the knife with smooth easy strokes, carving a pattern of flowers and leaves on the surface of the meat, the shed dark and cool around him, sunlight filtering through the spaces between the boards. Other carcasses hung on hooks nearby, each with the pattern on the leg. This was the last one. He took the caul from the lamb and flipped it out smooth, then wrapped it around the carcass. The caul, marbled with bits of fat, made a pattern like fine lace when he pressed it into the leaves and flowers. He had learned to do this from his tata in the old country. Every man had his own way to mark his work, to show that it was well done. And now the stores in town remembered him.

Today he was going on a big trip to sell lambs. First to Coteau and then to Regina. He hadn't liked to slaughter the yearling lambs, but he needed the money to pay Chisholm the rent for the land. It had been due the first of May, so he was a week late already. Chisholm had sent his sons over with a message: he wanted his money. And Stefan needed to buy flour, and cornmeal for mamaliga. He hung the last carcass on a hook and went in for breakfast.

Stefan was driving into Coteau for the first time since he had come to see the doctors. Then it had been bitterly cold, but today it was spring and the sun was warm on his face. Leaves were coming out on the few newly planted trees along the main street, grass was turning green in the schoolyard, and there were rowdy crows cawing in the big cottonwood by the Rowland Hotel. Stefan couldn't help glancing at the windows of the doctor's office as he drove by. He wondered what the doctor really felt in his own heart, and whether he was sorry about Trian. It was better if he could believe the doctor was sorry. He drove on down the street, past groups of children dawdling on their way to school and a few women out shopping. Without being told, Zaica stopped in front of Chan's store.

A woman stood at the counter buying meat, Chan on the other side serving her. Stefan got down and threw hay to Zaica, but didn't bother tying the horse to the railing in front of the store. He opened the door just as the woman was leaving. She seemed to shrink back against the door frame as she passed him. God knows why, he thought, I'm not going to grab her.

"Buna dimineatsa." Chan always greeted Stefan in his own language.

"Buna dimineatsa," Stefan answered.

Chan stood behind a big glass case full of meats. Along the side walls, rows of canned fruits and vegetables were stacked on wooden shelves, and in front of the counter a row of barrels contained flour, oatmeal, rice, cheese, tea, coffee, cornmeal. The place smelled of tea and spices. Chan turned and parted the curtain behind him, and Stefan followed him into the back room, filled with boxes and more shelves of canned food. No windows. In the centre of the room were a table and two chairs, a lighted lamp on the table. And a small iron heater where a blazing fire warmed a pot of rice and a china teapot on a scrolled iron stand. Chan brought the teapot and two small cups without handles, cups that fit smoothly into the palm of the hand. They sat down and Chan poured tea, strong and tarry, biting the tongue and coating the mouth. Warmth spread from the cup through Stefan's hands.

Even sitting, Chan looked tall. He was the tallest Chinese man Stefan had ever seen, a thin bony man with black hair turning grey, a wisp of long grey whiskers. Chan looked awkward until you saw him pour tea, his hands steady and strong. He brought the rice pot from the stove, a ladle, and two thin porcelain bowls painted with flowers. Not like the flowers in the old country or the pale prairie flowers of this new land, but brighter stronger colours. Chan filled the bowls with hot fluffy rice, handed Stefan chopsticks. They ate rice and drank tea that grew stronger and stronger.

Chan had dark eyes and big bony cheekbones that stuck out even more because he was so thin. Stefan's cheekbones slanted too, and he thought his olive skin made him look a little bit like the Chinese. "Son of a Tartar," his mother-in-law had called him. Chan filled the bowls again. Stefan could use chopsticks now almost as deftly as Chan, little wooden stilts in his hand. After rice, Chan emptied the last of the tea into the cups. Then he went to a high shelf at the back of the room and carefully lifted something down. He placed a wooden box on the table, an old and dirty box, but someone had made it carefully by hand. Chan opened it and took out a letter.

"Came last week," he said. With it were two photographs. One of a small boy about seven years old, and a second one in which a woman stood beside the same boy, smiling uncertainly. "My boy," Chan said, "my wife." Stefan studied the pictures. Although Chan must be nearly fifty years old, the woman couldn't be more than thirty-five. Her picture was not as clear as the boy's, she must have moved too soon. "Famous man from United States in my country to take pictures. My wife go to him for picture." Chan's wife and boy lived in Shanghai, but he himself came from Manchuria.

Stefan looked at the boy's picture again, the dark serious eyes, the hint of a smile around his lips, as though the mother were standing nearby speaking to him. The boy was only a few years older than Trian had been, and Stefan felt the force of Chan's longing for him.

"Looks like good boy," he said. "He will be tall like you." Already the boy was almost as tall as his mother.

"Very good boy," said Chan. "I save almost enough. Maybe this fall they come."

Chan hadn't seen his family for five years. His son had just been starting to talk when he left. He was saving to bring them to Canada, but it took a long time. The government made him pay lots of money, a head tax for each person, because they didn't want any more Chinese people to come.

Stefan remembered coming to Canada. The man who stamped their papers called them foreigners and tried to make them change their name to make it easier to write. He had learned that the government liked English people best, but they also needed people who could settle the land, even the poorest land, like the homestead at Fair View. Then foreigners were good enough, it seemed. He wondered how long the man who stamped the papers had been in Canada.

He looked again at the picture. "Real good boy," he said. He had planned to tell Chan about Trian, but he couldn't tell him now. Chan was slipping the pictures back into the letter and putting everything back into the box. Now it was time for business.

"Okay," said Chan, "I take three lamb. Four cent a pound."

Stefan shook his head. "Five cent. Very tender lambs."

Chan thought about it for a while, then nodded. "Okay, five."

Stefan unloaded the carcasses and Chan weighed them, hung them on hooks. They were about forty pounds each, low for market weight. Chan paid him six dollars. Stefan started to put the money away in his wallet, then stopped and handed back five. Chan had let him charge food over the winter. He couldn't take the money for the lambs and not pay what he owed, but he felt sick wondering if he could make enough for the rent. He tried to figure it out in his mind, but the numbers kept slipping away from him.

On the way out the door, Chan pressed something into Stefan's hand, a small painted jar of ginger. "For your wife," he said.

Chapter
FIVE

Zaica walked too slowly today. The stores closed in another hour, and already the owners would be grumpy. A poor time for bargaining. Just then they reached the top of a rise and suddenly Stefan could see the city.

Regina. Means queen, same as in the Romanian language. Very strange, Stefan thought, the capital city has a Romanian name. There sure was no queen here. No queen would want to live in such a place, with no beauty of any kind. It was named for the queen of England, the old one. The victorious one, same word as in Romanian. Dead now, but he'd seen pictures, a fat old baba, her clothes so tight she could hardly smile.

Coming into Regina, he looked back and found the whole south country hidden by the slight rise he'd just passed over. In all directions, the land appeared flat. He drove straight downtown, past houses as fine as the boyar's back in the village, past hotels and false-fronted stores. Some of the stores were larger than Chisholm's barn. But the store he was looking for was a one-storied whitewashed shop called "Vance's Meat Market." He stepped down from his wagon on to the wooden sidewalk. Someone clapped him on the shoulder.

"Stefan! Me tu! Stefan!" A wiry little man dressed all in black threw himself at Stefan, wrapping strong arms around him.

"Maica Domnului! Musca! Is that really you, Musca?" Stefan hugged him, slapped him on the back.

"Yes, Stefan, it's really me, Musca. Is it really you?"

"Asha, Musca! Of course it's me." Musca laughed and slapped Stefan's back. He hugged him and laughed a happy little laugh. People on the street turned to look.

"You're here, Stefan. I knew you would come at last."

"Me tu! Musca, what are you doing here? Why are you not in our village? I wrote you a letter in our village."

"I know, I know. I got the priest to read it for me." Stefan frowned. "Well, you know I have to get somebody, I can't read anything at all." Musca laughed at the idea of himself reading anything at all.

"Musca!" Stefan cried. "How is my mama?

My sisters? My little brother Alexandru?"

"Your mama, your sisters, they're all fine. Your little brother's not so little any more, and he's married."

"Alexandru? No — he's just a boy. Why did no one write to tell me?"

"That *boy's* bigger than you," Musca laughed. "And besides, somebody did write you." He stuck his chest out importantly.

"Maica Domnului, what strange things!"

"You see, I got your letter about the land here," Musca was saying. "How a man can make a little money if he knows how to look after sheep." Stefan looked embarrassed.

"Well, maybe it's not quite so good as all that."

"And I said to myself, Musca! Why are you sitting on your ass while your friend has gone to make lots of money in Ca-*na*-da? What kind of man are you? Are you stupid? Are you weak? No, Musca, I tell myself, you are quick like the fly. Does Musca the fly sit back while his friend goes to the new country and gets rich? For shame, Musca, I say. You must go and get rich too."

Musca grinned at Stefan, eyes like shiny brown berries beneath his dark eyebrows, dark skin wrinkled in laughing lines around his eyes. He wore dirty black trousers, a shapeless black jacket over a dark wool sweater. It made Stefan hot just to look at him.

"Listen, bun amic, we must go and have a drink right away—hey, hey, hey! I almost forgot." He laughed wickedly, turned his head this way and that to make sure no one was looking, then pulled a small bottle out of his coat. "Look, Stefan, I've got tsuica." He opened the half-empty bottle and handed it to Stefan, who looked embarrassed.

"Go on, drink! There's enough for both of us."

"Multsam, Musca, but it is against the law to drink in the street."

"Against the law?" Musca waved his arms to dismiss such a foolish law. "No, no, don't worry. To hell with them, eh? Drink, drink." Stefan looked around to see if anyone was watching them, then tipped the bottle and drank, and once again felt tsuica warming his throat. He handed it to Musca, who took a big swallow.

"Ah, that's good, eh? You can't get this stuff here. They don't know what it is." He handed the bottle to Stefan, who drank again.

"But Musca," he said, "why didn't you write that you were coming?"

"I did, six months ago. I got the priest to write for me."

"But we didn't get any letter. I bet it was that bastard priest. He hates me, you know."

"Ssssh! Stefan, don't talk like that. I saw him write the letter myself. He sits at his desk and he writes that I am coming, that I am going to be rich, that I say hello, that your mama says hello—"

Stefan suddenly saw his mama, as if she were standing in front of him, her tiny body, her hair that turned white the year before he left the old country.

"Musca," he asked, "didn't my mama send any message for me?"

"Me tu! I nearly forgot. She said it's too bad she won't see you again before she dies."

"My mama is dying?"

"Oh no, no, she'll last another twenty years. It's just her way of talking. You know these babas, they don't know anything about the world. They think if you leave the old country, that's that. It's like you're dead."

Stefan wanted to cry. His mama thought of him as dead. "And Sofie's mama and tata?"

"Oh, Stefan, they don't send a message by me. I'm not *good* enough for them." He seemed to be thinking that it served them right not to have a message carried if they thought he wasn't good enough.

Stefan's head was spinning. "Who did Alexandru marry?"

"You remember Yulka Muntean?"

"Little Yulka? Dina's sister?"

"That's the one, always had dirt on her nose. She's going to give Alexandru a little baby by harvest time."

Stefan shook his head. Musca linked an arm through his.

"Come on now, let's get a drink, and I'll tell you all about the village." Musca propelled him down the wooden sidewalk towards a hotel.

"Wait, Musca, I can't go just yet, I have things to do." They stopped in front of a door marked "Saloon."

"Let them wait, Stefan."

"No, you don't understand, I have to sell my lambs. I have no money." Musca thought about that.

"Where do you have to sell them?"

"Just back there — Vance's store." Stefan pointed.

"Okay," Musca said, "but first let's have more tsuica." He slid the bottle out of his coat, took a deep swallow. "Oh, that's good. Here, Stefan."

"No, later." Musca still held out the bottle, his berry eyes shining. "All right, just a little." He tipped it back and drank, not too much, he didn't want to look silly in front of Vance.

"Wait here," he said, "I'll be right back."

"Oh no, no," Musca said, "I'm coming with you. Then, you have any trouble, I'll be right there to help." He put his arm around Stefan and started him walking back to Vance's.

A bell tinkled and Vance looked up from his counter as they walked in. Stefan, carrying one of the dressed lambs, felt a bit unsteady on his feet.

Damn, he'd forgotten how strong tsuica was. Musca hung back near the door, his black eyes on the funny English man. Stefan smiled.

"Yes," said Vance warily, "what can I do for you?"

"I come to sell lambs," Stefan said.

"Oh yes, Mr. Dominescu, isn't it? How many did you bring?"

"Seven, about forty to fifty pound each one."

"Watch out, Stefan," Musca said in Romanian, "this bugger would cheat his own baba."

"What did your friend say?"

"He say... you have a good store here," Stefan lied. Musca snickered and Vance threw him a dirty look. Stefan lay the lamb carcass down on the counter. Vance looked it over.

"Very nice," he said. "Four and a half cents a pound." Musca snorted.

"Six," Stefan suggested.

"Six? Oh no, six is way out of line."

"Six."

"That's telling him," Musca said in Romanian, "this guy'd skin a flea for its hide." Vance glared. Stefan tried not to laugh.

"Look, it's impossible. I'd be doing you a favour at five."

"Five cent I can get at Coteau. Why I should come so far, make my horse tired, waste feed, just for same price I get at Coteau from Chinaman?"

"That right," Musca said in English.

Vance took a deep breath. He spoke very slowly and clearly as if Stefan would have trouble understanding:

"How many stores in Coteau?"

"One."

"Will it buy all the lambs you've got to sell?"

"No, he don't need so much."

"Okay, so you come to the city to sell. But here we have many stores selling meat. People go around to see who has the best price. I have to keep the price low, so people will come to my store. Understand?"

"Oh, oh," Musca said in their language, "this doesn't look so good."

Vance couldn't stand it. "Does your friend have to jabber away like that?" Musca looked offended.

"Musca," Stefan said in Romanian, "perhaps it would be better if only I spoke with the man."

"But I'm only trying to help."

"I know, my friend, but it will go more quickly if only one of us speaks."

"Oh, all right." Musca stuck out his lower lip.

Vance put his hands in the pockets of his white coat, stained with blood from the meat he cut up. "Five cents is all I can pay if I'm going to make any money." Stefan nodded gravely.

"I see. You want people come to your store, so you must offer good price."

"That's right. Now you've got it."

Stefan looked thoughtful. "These people, they like meat that is good, nice and fat, tender?"

"Yes, they like those things."

"People come back your store if they get always good meat?"

"Yes, yes, we like to sell only the best meat," Vance said impatiently. Musca snickered, Vance glared. Stefan stared hard at Musca: *Shut up*, he was thinking.

Stefan smiled at Vance. "Well then," he said reasonably, "might be worth it pay little more for good meat, no?" Vance looked annoyed, Musca was snickering soundlessly into his hands. "These lamb I bring, they very good. People buy them, they come back to your store, no? I think maybe these lamb worth six cent."

Musca nodded his head vigorously, his face a mask of glee. "You tell him, Stefan," he said.

"Musca," Stefan said quietly, "shut up."

"Look, I'm telling you the truth," Vance said. "Five cents is the most you'll get anywhere in town today."

"And I tell you, mister, I take these lamb home and feed my own family before I sell for five cent." He stared into the butcher's eyes. Musca was dancing up and down with excitement, but keeping his mouth shut. Stefan moved to carry away the carcass he'd brought in to show. Vance looked at it, then at Stefan.

"Wait," he said. Stefan stopped. "Five and a half." Musca rubbed his hands together, gave a little hop.

"Okay," Stefan said. "Five and a half. If you take all."

"All right, all right, it's a deal."

Musca clapped him on the back, laughing. Together they went back to the wagon and carried the lambs in. Vance weighed the carcasses, wrote numbers on a piece of paper. He paid Stefan seventeen dollars and fifty cents. Even with the other dollar from Chan, it wasn't enough for the payment, and he still needed supplies. There were no more lambs big enough to butcher. If he hadn't paid Chan — but he'd had to pay him. His stomach felt sick, and it seemed he'd known all along he wouldn't be able to pay.

The bell tinkled again as they went out, Musca's arm around Stefan. Stefan tucked his purse inside his jacket, closed the pocket with a button. No one could get at it without him knowing, but he planned to pat it now and then just to make sure.

"That was some deal you made, Stefan," Musca was saying. "That Vance didn't know what to say."

A good deal, yes, but he couldn't pay his rent. And he realized now what he should have done. Why hadn't he agreed to five cents but asked for Vance to give him groceries wholesale? Shit, he was stupid.

"Now let's have a drink," Musca pleaded.

Stefan stopped at Merryman's Grocery, bought sacks of flour and cornmeal and half a pound of peppermints. He now had fifteen dollars.

"Now, bun amic, now we have a drink?"

"All right," Stefan agreed, "now we have a drink."

The table was covered with glasses of beer. "So I get off the train here, I look around and there's nobody. It's raining hard — my boots were nice and new then — and all there is here is mud. I thought, Jesus Christ, Musca, you're on your own now, not even your old mama knows where you are today. I couldn't see what I was going to do. Not much money. No one meeting me."

"It's the priest, I tell you," Stefan said.

"The first night I felt pretty bad. I took my bag and walked out into the country till I came to a place where there was a few trees, and I made myself a camp. At first I was afraid of fantoma, but I couldn't hear anything. I had nothing to eat, except in my bag a little piece of cheese, that I bought in Winnipeg to eat on the train. And some water from a pond near the trees. Ugh, filthy!" He stopped to drink, drained the glass.

"Were you very cold, sleeping in the grass?"

"Cold? Of course I was cold. This is one cold country. But what is that, to be a little cold, eh? And I did have a small sheepskin in my bag... Anyway, I *live*, and when morning comes, I splash some water on my face. Musca, I say, you have to go into that town and get some work. Must be something you can do in this Queen town to make a little money." The waiter came with more beer, and Stefan paid because Musca was busy talking. "Maybe then you can go find out what happened to your friend Stefan." Stefan looked embarrassed.

"So I'm walking back to town, and a farmer gives me a ride in his wagon. He goes to a stable where people leave their horses when they come to town, and what do you think I see?" He drained a glass.

"What do you see, Musca Graba?"

"There is no one to take the horse. I try to ask the man who owns the stable if he wants someone to help. I point to myself and make signs to him—leading horses, feeding horses, grooming horses. And me tu! I got myself a job. For now, he lets me sleep in the loft, and I get enough money to eat, buy some beer at night. But I'm getting a bit lonely here by myself. I'm sure glad to see you."

"And I'm glad to have found you, my fast one. You were very brave to come so far alone."

"Yes, wasn't I? The joke is, I didn't know how alone I was going to be!" He slapped his thigh. "Or maybe I wouldn't have been so brave."

"Now that I've found you, you must come visit us."

"That would be very fine, but I can't leave my horses just yet —"

"And Kosma and Nina Manescu, you must visit them too."

"Kosma! Asha, I would like to see my old friend. And your woman? How is she?"

"Sofie is very well," Stefan said, suddenly feeling very tired.

"And your children? Luba and Nicu, and little Trian?"

Stefan put down the glass of beer. For the first time since Trian's death, he'd forgotten for a short while.

"Musca," he said, "Trian is dead."

"Dead, bun amic, how? I never heard."

"I never wrote anybody. I was too ashamed."

"Ashamed?"

Stefan told the story as simply as he could, while the tears flowed down Musca Graba's cheeks.

"I am sorry, Stefan. I never heard of such a thing, not even in the old country." He patted Stefan's sleeve. "Ah, your poor woman, how is she taking it?"

"She blames me. She tries not to, but all the

same, she blames me."

"Oh no," Musca crooned, "she blames you. That is very bad." He wiped tears on his sleeve.

"Sofie will have another baby in the fall," Stefan said. "But she cannot stop grieving for Trian. And she wishes she were back in the old country."

Musca looked horrified. "Oh no, no, Stefan, better to stay here. A man can make more money here. Like you, already lots of land, good house. Like a boyar."

Stefan spoke very low. "I only rent the land, and the house is small."

"But three bedrooms, that is something, eh? Your mama told me."

Stefan stared at the beer. So he'd fibbed a bit — whoever thought anyone from the village would ever come all this way to see? Now everyone would know his failure on the homestead, the poor place he lived in, and the shame of Trian's death.

"You know, Stefan, I missed you a lot." Musca was trying to cheer him up. "Yes, I used to have more fun when you were around."

Stefan tried to smile. "You should have found some nice girl, got married."

"What girl would marry poor Graba?" Musca asked. "Don't let him touch me! He eats flies!" he cried, mimicking a mincing girl's voice. Now Stefan couldn't help smiling.

"Yes, my friend, we had some good times. When we were boys, no thought of girls or marriage, no worries, just looking after our fathers' sheep, helping ourselves to the village gardens—"

"Stefan! Me tu!" Musca's face lit up. "Do you remember the pears? The pears of old man Radu?"

"Do I remember! Old man Somnoros we called him afterwards."

"Ah, the pears, so beautiful and round." Musca sighed.

"And so ripe and juicy, Musca."

"Yes, so ripe and juicy." Musca closed his eyes in ecstasy, softly rubbing his stomach. "Could anyone really have blamed us, considering how ripe and juicy they were?"

"And more than old man Somnoros could eat, even with his old baba."

"Oh, many more, Stefan, we agreed they could never eat them all. There was enough for a whole village."

"And too, he was so very careless of them."

"Oh, very careless. It was almost an invitation."

"There he lay, in the long grass, in the shade of one of his beautiful trees."

"Sleeping so peacefully, Stefan, like a baby. And his snoring, so loud and strong." He laughed. "Like thunder... to say nothing of his bashina." They laughed, remembering old man

Radu's farts.

"Doamne! his farts were very fine, the old man loved his garlic. But they were soon lost in the fresh air, filled with the smell of ripe pears."

Musca looked thoughtful. "It wasn't that we were very hungry, really."

"No, it was more to see if we could do it, but those pears were sure good eating."

"Very good eating," Musca agreed. "So there is me and you and Kosma, creeping past the old man. We picked the juiciest and the best pears. Any with bruises we threw away. If some insect had eaten from them, we threw that away too. We flipped the cores past his head."

Stefan laughed out loud at the memory. "And each time we're standing there ready to run. We thought he'd catch on right away, but no, he just kept snoring on, his chest gently rising and falling. A beautiful old man, that Somnoros Radu. Snowy hair and beard curling around his face. Like some patriarch in the Bible." They took deep drinks from their beer.

"Beautiful," Musca agreed. "We sat and watched him sleep. Kosma kept snickering." They laughed. "We thought for sure he'd wake up then, but he must have thought it was just his own farts. It wasn't pears he was eating that day!"

They could hardly talk, felt weak with laughing. "And then... and then, Musca my fly, you said you thought you knew what would wake him up! Oh, how we admired your balance... your nerve! That was when we knew you were a brave one. What skill—"

"Balanced over his open hand—"

"We were ready to run, but you had your pants down, and so beautifully balanced, so well aimed, you—"

"Shit in his hand!" They exploded in laughter. They were getting louder and louder, and other people turned to look at them. "And Stefan, he... didn't even wake up!" Waves of laughter rolled over them. "He didn't even move. His chest just went a little faster for a few breaths, and then came the snoring again."

"So then, Musca, we began to wonder if anything will wake this man up. We could see he was alive, but it looks like nothing will wake him." Stefan pressed his sides, to hold in the laughter. "So we started thinking. I got long stalks of grass, one for each of us. Then, oh so gently, we brush them across his face, at first so softly he'd dream of the breeze touching him. Then a little more just to tickle, along his forehead, along his nose. And then we get ready to run. He moves a little, the muscles in his arm twitch." Stefan mimicked the old man's face, twitched his arm.

"And then," Musca grabbed Stefan's arm, "and then, it's too much for him, there's some insect, a fly, on his face, he's going to kill it, teach it a real lesson, and we brushed the grass across his face again, just a little harder. Suddenly his arm moved, and... and... splat!" Musca broke up in loud laughter.

"And then we started to run, but we didn't need to because... because he couldn't see a thing anyway." Stefan, too, collapsed with laughter. He felt so weak and his head was light and giddy and he knew he was drunk, was forgetting again, but it felt so good...

"All right, you two, that's enough!" said a loud voice, "Out!"

"What iss wrong?" Stefan asked weakly, but he had trouble making his mouth shape the English words.

"Out! We don't need rowdies here," and someone lifted them both from their seats, he was a big man, and they were so weak with laughing. "Out!" Without meaning to, they found themselves walking towards the door, a firm hand at each of their backs. Musca, still laughing, asked, "What's the matter with this asshole anyway?" and Stefan thought how nice it was that English people don't understand Romanian.

"Wait," Stefan tried again, "what is wrong?"

"Out!" the man cried, "and stay out!" and as they were floating through the door, he gave them both a good push that sent them stumbling out into the warm evening, but they didn't fall down, caught themselves in time. "You always did have good balance," Stefan said, "just like a fly," and they broke into fresh waves of laughter.

"You know," Musca said, "that was the only time my old tata beat me. I never saw him so goddamn mad."

"Funny thing," Stefan said, "how they knew it was us." Roaring with laughter, they staggered arm in arm down the street.

Stefan began to think he should start for home. His head felt so light and it would be getting dark soon. He should get home, he was drunk and he was forgetting about Trian. A terrible thought struck him. He had left Zaica and the wagon with the supplies in front of Vance's store. What if someone had stolen them? Then he laughed out loud. Who would bother to steal a horse like Zaica?

He thought he should ask Musca to come and stay with them. But Sofie wouldn't like it.

"That filthy Musca!" she would say. "He eats flies."

"Not any more," he would tell her, "that was just once, because the boys teased him." Musca's real name was Florian, and the boys called him "Floricica"—little flower. He only ate flies once to show them he was tough. But Sofie never believed it. Once you ate flies, you always ate flies, and flies were part of your skin and hair and flesh and teeth.

"You should come home with me now, Musca, visit a while. Then maybe you could go see Kosma, help him with his harvest." If only there was some way Musca would refuse, at least until he got Sofie used to the idea.

"That would be good, my friend. But not this time, eh?"

"But why not, Musca, you are all alone here." Now that Musca didn't want to come right away, Stefan felt hurt.

"Well, you see, the man at the stables, he depends on me. He can't get another man so fast." Musca looked embarrassed.

"Oh come on, Musca. Come and visit."

"Besides, Stefan, it would be quite a surprise for your woman. She doesn't even know I'm here. Sometimes the women don't like something so sudden."

"That is true. Sofie is going to have a baby in the fall and she is not feeling so good. Perhaps it would be better if I prepared her for this good news."

"That's right, my friend, prepare her. Then, another time, when you come to town, I will come for a visit."

"All right, Musca. Another time you will come." They had reached Vance's store, and there was the wagon, and the supplies, and there was Zaica, sound asleep on his feet.

A woman walked towards them, and just as

she passed on the sidewalk, she turned her body slightly towards them. "Hello there, boys, and where are you going so fast?"

Stefan was stunned. Women here didn't talk to him. He wanted to laugh because she said they were going fast, and really they had stopped, and she couldn't know that his friend was Graba, the fast one. She stopped beside them on the sidewalk.

"Hell-oo thay-er," Musca was talking to the woman in English, almost as if he knew her, "how yoo air?"

"Just fine, honey, just fine." She moved a little closer to Musca. "Who's your friend there, he looks kind of sweet." She looked boldly at Stefan, and he felt he was blushing, the blush flowing all the way down to his crotch in a warm wave. He saw now that the woman's dress was a little too low in front, and he thought he saw paint on her cheeks.

"Thees my friend, Stefan," Musca said, winking broadly from behind the woman's back.

"You boys doing anything tonight?" she asked. Stefan blushed again. Sofie would kill him if she knew.

"I must... I have to go now," he answered, "I have a long way to go." But he couldn't help looking at her. What kind of woman was it who made love with any man who came along? He realized he was staring, and his cheeks felt hot.

"You wouldn't like to go for a drink, would you, Mr. Stefan?" She smiled at him, in the most brazen way, she was asking *him*, looking right into his eyes. Maica Domnolui, what was he going to say?

"Thank you very much... " he hesitated, Musca was making faces at him, "but—" And then he wanted to go with her. Why not? Why should Sofie care? Sofie blamed him. He felt the warmth again in his belly and crotch, wanted to say yes to the woman. He still had some of the money, why not have what he wanted? Stefan made himself look away from the teasing eyes, made himself think about Sofie and the baby coming in the fall. His baby. "Thank you very much," he said, "but I must go home." He said the words, but they left a sour taste in his mouth, like the taste of the beer.

She turned to the grinning Musca. "What about you, big boy?" Stefan laughed; how could anyone call Musca "big"? Musca was looking into her eyes.

"That very *goood*," he said. The woman linked her arm through his, ready to walk away. Musca leaned towards Stefan, spoke low in Romanian.

"Lend me a dollar, bun amic."

"What?"

"A dollar. Lend me a dollar. You know, amic, the money of this place. Lend me some quickly, and I will remember you always." He held his hand out a little impatiently.

"Asha, I see," Stefan said, and reached into his hidden pocket, which he noticed was unbuttoned, and got out his purse. He saw that he had already spent nearly two dollars on beer. Only thirteen left. He took out another dollar and handed it to Musca, who was still grinning and winking.

"Multsam, my friend, multsam," Musca patted Stefan's arm with his free hand. "I must go now, but next time you come to town, I will be happy to go back to your place for a visit." The woman looked impatient at this foreign talk, tapped her foot against the boards of the sidewalk.

"Let's go, then," she said, tugging at Musca's arm. He winked again at Stefan, and shrugged his shoulders, as if to show that there was nothing he could do if women were crazy about him.

"Good-bye," he said, walking off with the woman. "Until our visit."

"Good-bye," Stefan called after Musca's retreating back. Musca turned to wave and give one last wicked wink. Stefan thought of the long drive home and felt very tired. He thought of the woman, friendly and smiling, not like Sofie at home, still brooding. Almost all the light had gone from the sky.

Zaica was still sleeping. Stefan rattled the harness to wake him up.

Chapter
SIX

She sat in her new rocker, the smooth wooden back and seat rounded to the shape of her body. Stefan had made it from clean new wood he bought in town, golden wood with just a touch of red, with wavy patterns through it like rippling water. As he'd worked on it, through the coldest months of winter, the house had been filled with the smell of summer forests, and it had made her think of the old country.

Sofie liked the way the arms of the rocker supported her own arms when she sat knitting. The tops of the arms were curved and smooth, but along the sides and underneath, Stefan had carved pictures in the wood, flowers and animals and little birds, remembered from their old village. The rockers were the same, crusted on the sides with leaves, branches, birds. Her favourite was a baby owl, perched on a branch, peering out at her with a funny half-angry look. So serious. Trian had looked like that when he was thinking about something he didn't understand. Little baliuna, she'd called him. Little owl.

Here the owls lived in holes in the ground. Sofie loved to watch birds, to follow their quick neat movements. With spring the birds had come back, and their singing seemed to bring the land back to life. But she remembered the thick green grass in their old village and was not consoled.

One morning as Sofie was getting out of bed, she thought she saw Trian. He was standing by the bed, and she knew he was going to speak to her. She had the feeling he wanted to tell her about where he was now. Then she heard Stefan calling her name and she turned to answer him; when she looked again, Trian was gone.

And now she was pregnant again, but she didn't feel glad as she had with the others. She didn't want another baby, could never replace Trian with another baby. Even so, she was knitting a baby dress as she rocked, the wool soft against her fingers, the best and silkiest fleece, spun as fine as she could with her hand spindle. She used her thinnest needles, straining her eyes over stitches that looked like a band of lace. Sofie liked to make pretty things, and she was proud of her work.

The winter had been long and hard. Hard on the ewes giving birth in the snow. Hard on lambs that were too small or too sickly to survive. Winter tired her, left too much time for thoughts to come into her head. Hard thoughts. You could put them away for a while, but they always came back. Especially at night, when she and Stefan worked in the light of the coal oil lamp. Now it was spring at last, but a drab, dry spring with only the pale crocuses blooming along the hillsides. Even now the children found banks of musty snow melting in the coulees. The chill of winter was still there in her bones, and she longed for summer, to feel warm again clear through.

She looked at Stefan, sitting in a chair by the table, his dark head bent over the work in his hands. He was braiding strips of leather, seven of them, making a belt for Nicu. Nicu didn't need another belt yet, but Stefan had the leather, and it was something to do. She watched his brown hands weaving the soft leather, his face becoming smooth as the work filled his mind. The only sounds were the rocking of her chair and the sounds of breathing. Sofie sighed. She didn't like this room. The walls were too close, the windows too small. It had been Chisholm's first house in Canada, and he'd built it small and cheap; he must have known he'd have a better one some day. Sofie was angry with the windows, although it was foolish to be angry at things. She wanted to cut into the walls, make bigger windows, so they could see out across the hills. She had been angry with the windows ever since the day last fall when they first came to this place. She remembered stopping at the Chisholms' for the key.

The Chisholm house was made from stone, cut in blocks. The blocks were square and blunt, marked like roughly hewn wood by the tool which had cut them. It was the biggest house she'd ever seen, big as the monastery back in the village. But not as beautiful.

She couldn't understand how you cut stone; wouldn't it break any blade? They said Chisholm himself cut the rocks. That was his work in the country he came from. A useful trade in a country with no forests. If there is no wood, you must make a house out of rocks, a house cold and dark like a cave.

Stefan jumped down from the wagon, his movements quick and sharp. He thinks they may be watching him, she thought. She herself sat straighter, pulling her shawl closer to keep out the October chill. She saw a woman's face for a moment at one of the windows, like a pale thin moon, then it was gone. Stefan reached the door, it opened, and there was a man, short and stocky with light hair the colour of sand, his skin freckled with patches of the same colour. Like the spots on an old woman's hands. Chisholm. He watched as Stefan spoke, eyes narrow and untrusting, as if Stefan were a gypsy offering him a horse. Then he turned and went back into the *dark shadows of the house. Stefan waited. The man came back and handed something to Stefan. The key. Stefan was speaking. Chisholm gave a sharp nod, shut the door in his face.*

She wanted Stefan to look at her, but he drove off with his eyes straight ahead, flapped the reins hard. Zaica tried to go a little faster, the wheels grinding against the gravel as they passed Chisholm's barns and sheds. Sofie stared at the barn, bigger and taller than the house, its roof reaching high like the roof of a church. Its foundation matched the stone blocks of the house. The wooden walls were pure white, not whitewashed, but painted with real paint from the store. She couldn't guess the cost of that much paint. And for a barn! The dull green roof also matched the roof of the house, and all the other sheds and granaries were painted in the same colours. In a pasture beside the barn, some ewes grazed, purebred Romneys, along with two fawn coloured Jersey cows. Sofie thought about the milk those cows would give, the thick yellow cream.

At the bottom of the hill Chisholm's road turned sharply back to the main road they had travelled from Fair View and the burnt-up land of their homestead. They were never going back to the homestead. Four hard dry years, and nothing to show for it. Sofie had laughed bitterly when they told her what Fair View meant.

Stefan didn't even look at the turnoff, but kept driving south. There was no gravel here, just a faint trail through a long coulee. The land was rough, hillier than at Fair View. Sofie looked up at hills that cut off the view of everything beyond, hills studded with jagged boulders, their bases buried in the earth. The land itself was mixed with pebbles and stones. Land you could never plough. Badlands, they called it.

Stefan didn't speak. It hurt his pride to deal with Chisholm. Chisholm knew they were hard up, they had to take his terms. He didn't want them to be like neighbours. He treated them like hired help. He didn't know — her father had the best house in the village. They were as good as Chisholm.

They came to a gravel pit cut into a hill, spilling stones down the hillside, across the trail. The wagon jolted, and Sofie quickly glanced back at the children. It was all right, Luba held tightly to Trian. Nicu was watching a clump of stunted trees near the pit, where two crows circled. She hated crows, their hoarse cries made her shiver. Past the gravel pit was their land, rented from Chisholm. They were coming out of the long coulees, the road curving around the base of a huge hill. Rounding the curve, they saw the house, about half-way up the hill.

It was a shack, grey and worn as the one they'd left behind, with a broken-down lean-to porch in front. The smashed porch window showed only blackness, the house seemed set against them. They all climbed down from the wagon, and Nicu and Luba began to walk to the top of the hill. But Trian stayed close to Sofie. The lean-to door stood ajar, its crude leather latch long since rotted through, the porch full of junk from the hired men who'd lived there before—bits of lumber, a hammer with a broken claw, rusty cooking pots, a broken pump handle splintered along the bottom. Sofie stepped around these things, seeing herself throwing them all out, as Stefan opened the padlock of the inner door.

The kitchen looked very dark, and she hesitated, listening for the scrabbling steps of mice or rats. She peered in at walls, whitewashed long ago, streaked now with soot where a pipe had leaked. Her eyes followed the pipe to a stove, a wood-burning cookstove as wide as her arms stretched out. Stefan tore open the curtains, and Sofie stared at the stove. It was black, trimmed with silvery metal in curling shapes, scrolls of metal in the corners, along the door of the warming oven, on the rounded feet. Now it was covered with thick grease, furry with dust, but when it was cleaned and polished—Doamne! These English could make something beautiful after all.

The children ran ahead up the narrow stairs.

"Look mama, see how many rooms!" Trian said. Three small rooms upstairs, to be used only for sleeping. Trian didn't seem to see the dirt, the smallness. Sofie noticed the musty smell, like old wet sawdust. She was sure there must be mice.

In the biggest bedroom, the one for the parents, was a double iron bedstead, sagging mattress soiled an even grey, marked with faded brown stains. Her stomach churned. Thank God they had their own straw mattresses. Most likely these had bedbugs. She would throw them out and wipe the bed frames with kerosene. That would kill the dirty bugs. Trian reached out a hand towards the mattress.

"Me tu! Stop!" she cried. "Don't touch that, it's filthy!" His brown eyes stared up at her. She had never spoken to him so sharply, and he began to cry.

Sofie's throat burned. How could she have spoken so unkindly? She stopped rocking, and Stefan looked up at her. She pushed the tears back down and held her face still. She started to rock again. But now she could hold the thoughts back no longer. Once more she saw the doctors arriving. Their big fur coats made them look like big men, but when they took them off, she was surprised to see how thin they seemed. She saw them go up the stairs like smoke in the chimney. Then they came down and talked about how they must take out Trian's tonsils. And Stefan said yes. He said yes.

She saw Trian's head on her lap, her hand stroking his face. She saw the blood welling from his mouth, black in the dark room. How odd that was, that the blood seemed to be black. It trickled slowly across his cheek, wetting her skirt. She felt the cold spot with her hand.

And she saw the doctors leaving, and herself trying to hold them back, to ask questions. "You like to have some supper with us?" she asked them, but they were already putting on their coats. Then they seemed like big men again. "You like some supper?" she had asked again, ashamed of her poor English. And the young one had smiled at her. He had smiled. Jesus Christ! she thought, they killed my boy, and I asked them to eat with us. She wanted to tear at her hair, to scratch her nails across her face.

The rocking chair was still. She wouldn't cry, but her face and throat were tight with pain that came up through her in waves until she thought she wouldn't be able to breathe. Then Stefan was beside her, bending over her. She wouldn't look into his face. He took the knitting from her hands, put it on the table.

"Let yourself cry, Sofie. Draga, let yourself cry." He put an arm around her shoulders, stroked her rounding belly. She wanted to turn to him, but she didn't know if she could ever truly forgive him. The thoughts would always come back, and then she would think: he let them do it.

"Come to bed now, dragutsa. Come to bed." He tugged gently at her arm, but she pulled it away.

Chapter
SEVEN

Stefan stepped carefully on the narrow path, gravel shifting beneath his feet, May sun hot on his head. At the front door he stopped, checked the soles of his boots, then knocked on the heavy oak door. Out of the corner of his eye he saw a face peeking out of a downstairs window. When he turned, it was gone. In a moment the door opened, and Mrs. Chisholm stood partly concealed behind it, a tall woman in a tight black dress. A faint smile touched her lips.

"Good morning," Stefan said.

"Good morning," she said. "It's Mr. Dominescu, isn't it?"

"Yes. I come to see Mr. Chisholm."

"He's just gone to the gravel pit with the boys." Stefan nodded. "He's afraid the road will wash out one of these days with all the rain." She hadn't asked him in, or opened the door any wider.

"I am hoping to see him... I have some business."

Mrs. Chisholm looked uncomfortable. She clasped her hands together, stroking her gold wedding ring with the thumb of her right hand. "I'm expecting him back soon, he said he would come to the house for coffee." She took a deep breath. "Would you like to come in and wait for him?"

"Yes, please. That is fine." She stepped back and Stefan followed her in. They were in a large dimly-lit hall, with doors leading to other rooms, and a staircase at the far end.

She looked embarrassed. "Come in and have a cup of coffee," she said, leading him to the kitchen.

Here it was much brighter, with windows facing south, curtained in yellow gingham, letting in light and warmth. A table and chairs stood in front of the windows, the table covered in shiny yellow oilcloth. Sofie would like this room. Mrs. Chisholm motioned him to a chair, and went to the stove for coffee. She brought two cups, sat down across from him. She held her cup in her right hand, while the fingers of the left clenched and unclenched. She seemed to be searching for something to say.

"Well," she said finally, "it's been a hard winter." Her eyes flickered across his face as she spoke, then slid away.

"Yes," he said, "a hard winter."

She couldn't keep her hands still. They would smooth down her skirt, or touch her gold wedding band, then move away again, hovering like clumsy birds. He drank coffee, trying not to stare at those hands, so pale and small, across the table from his own dark hands. He looked at her face, young still in spite of the grey streaks in the black hair, the lines around her mouth and eyes. She took small shallow breaths as if sipping the air. At the sound of a wagon, her head turned sharply to the window.

Stefan saw Chisholm standing near the barn, talking to his sons, pointing to the load of gravel, then the road. His fingers jabbed the blue morning air. The boys nodded slowly, and Chisholm turned and strode towards the house. Mrs. Chisholm went to the stove and pretended to be busy, moving the coffee pot around, checking something in the warming oven. Stefan watched Chisholm through the window. He was short and stocky, with a bullish strength massed in his heavy arms and shoulders. His sandy hair, cut short, pale blue eyes and short snubbed nose gave him a blunt unfinished look. He carried himself stiffly, even in his own yard. You never knew when somebody might be trying to put one over on you, or so his body seemed to be saying.

Chisholm came in the side door, which opened into the kitchen. He started when he saw Stefan seated at the table, coffee cup in hand.

The pale eyes narrowed, turned to his wife. Her cheeks reddened, her eyes pleaded: What could I do? I had to ask him in, didn't I? He's a neighbour, isn't he? His look was just as clear: not neighbours, foreigners.

Chisholm turned to Stefan. "Morning, Mr. Dominescu," he said casually. "Come to pay your rent, have you? You're late." He glanced at his hands, which were dirty, and at the enamelled washbasin on the cupboard. His wife hurried to fetch water from the stove reservoir.

"Good morning, Mr. Chisholm. I want to talk about deal I make with you." Chisholm went on soaping his hands with great concentration, covering them in thick foamy lather.

"Aye," he said, without looking up, "go on, I'm listening." The rain water was so soft, he couldn't rinse all the suds off.

"I want to ask, can you wait a little for the money? Spring very late this year, very cold. Many lamb get sick and die. And now I must buy feed for my sheep."

He stopped, staring as Mrs. Chisholm brought a pitcher of clear warm water and poured it over Chisholm's outstretched hands, gave him a clean towel to dry with. Then she put everything away, took the basin of dirty water outside to throw away.

"Aye," said Chisholm, "that's so. I've lost a good many lambs myself." Stefan did not reply at once. "I say, I've lost a good many myself. Times are hard for everybody." He spoke loudly, as if Stefan had difficulty hearing. He seated himself at the table across from Stefan, then turned and looked hard at his wife, who hurried over with coffee and rolls. Nothing more was offered to Stefan.

"Your sheep are your own affair, Mr. Dominescu. I told you that when you came here. You rent the land for them, you buy the feed. And at shearing time, I'll pay you the going rate for your help. In the meantime, don't complain to me if the winter is long. You should have thought of that before you left wherever it was." He took a careful swallow of the scalding coffee. "Times are hard for everyone," he repeated.

"That is true, Mr. Chisholm," Stefan answered. "But can you wait a little time for the money? I pay when I shear my sheep."

Chisholm spread his cinnamon roll with a thick slab of butter; he broke it neatly in half, held one half poised in each hand. "And who is to pay my rent?" he asked. "I have to pay Mr. Rowland his due, or he'll be down on my neck like a hawk on a fieldmouse. You don't think old man Rowland would wait, do you? Well? Who's going to pay *my* rent?" He began to eat the roll, chewing hard, thoroughly.

Chisholm already owned plenty of land, but he wanted more. He was renting from the Rowlands, building up more holdings for his sons. And as Mr. Rowland was doing to Chisholm, Chisholm was determined to do to him, Stefan. "You are here on this ranch many year," he said. "I thought maybe you are able to wait for this money." Mrs. Chisholm stood by the stove, not looking at Stefan or her husband. Chisholm washed the piece of roll down with coffee, took another big bite. He's right, Stefan thought, I should have taken more care before I came all this way. Never to have to deal with landlords again, that was what they promised. At least at home we knew what to expect. Here they only pretend one man is as good as another. This Chisholm reminded him more and more of that zmeu, that devil of a boyar back in the village. He stood up to leave.

Chisholm raised his hand. "Wait," he said, wiping some crumbs from around his mouth, "there may be a way I can help you." Stefan sank back to his seat. He waited.

"I think I can cancel your payment entirely." Stefan listened, kept his face still. What was the man saying? "In return," Chisholm was saying, and Stefan saw a little movement of fear in Mrs. Chisholm's face, "in return, you will do some work for me. You will do my spring shearing," his pallid eyes looked into Stefan's, "you and your boy." Stefan clenched his fists. This was not part of their agreement.

"You will do my spring shearing. When I'm ready, even if you'd rather be doing your own. A thousand sheep."

A thousand sheep. He could make at least fifty dollars for that work if he hired on a shearing crew. His arms tightened, he wanted to take the cup of hot coffee and throw it in the man's face. He thought of Sofie; he couldn't do that. Mrs. Chisholm stood by the stove, not moving.

"Mr. Chisholm," he said finally, "you want me to shear all your sheep for twenty dollar?" Chisholm nodded, eyes fixed on Stefan, chewing another mouthful of his roll, gulping his coffee.

"But I can pay you this money after I shear my own sheep!"

"Aye, Mr. Dominescu, you could. But the payment is due now. Who is to pay me for waiting? You people don't seem to understand, I could have that money in the bank now, earning interest. The payment is late as it is." He raised his broad hand as Stefan made a slight movement towards the door. "So if you want my help, you must give me something of value for it." He brushed crumbs from his fingers and sat facing Stefan. "It is a great deal of work, but you're used to it. You and your boy."

Stefan held his face still, wouldn't let Chisholm see anything from his eyes. He tried to come up with one other way. Kosma? Chan? Kosma had no money to spare, and Chan was saving to bring his family to Canada.

"I agree. Write it on paper." He saw rather than heard Mrs. Chisholm's slow sigh of relief.

"Aye," said Chisholm, and looked at his wife. She brought him a pen and paper, a bottle of black ink.

Chapter
EIGHT

It was going to be hot, but there was still coolness in the morning air, in the dewy tufts of grass around the big corral. Chisholm and his boys had driven all their sheep into the fenced pasture behind the corral early in the morning, and they'd gone out to fix fence. Sheep crowded together, like a hummocky white sea, till you couldn't see the ground. Like a field of giant cauliflowers. Nicu laughed at the thought.

Nicu looked at his father. The bones seemed to stand out in the thin tanned face, glistening with fine sweat. Tata worked without a pause, never seeming to hurry, so smooth you hardly saw how fast he worked. Nicu tried to do the same. He could almost close his eyes and shear sheep. At night when he tried to sleep, it would all be there: the woolly coats, the ache in his back, his feet braced against the soft packed earth, crowding every other thing from his mind. Without looking, he could see and feel his hands, saturated with grease that wouldn't wash off at night. The grease was good, it helped protect his skin from the sharp grass and burrs stuck to the wool. Even so, his hands were cut and scratched.

The sheep looked so funny when he let them go. They would stand nervously against the fence, ridiculously light and hairless, ready to run away this time — you weren't going to fool them twice. They'd move jerkily around the corral, not quite sure they were still themselves, but really feeling the soft summer air. Nicu looked at the sheep in the pasture. There always seemed to be as many as when they started. He could only measure their work by the shorn sheep in the corral. Tata would shear more than sixty sheep by the end of the day. He hoped to do nearly fifty himself. At night the Chisholm boys would drive the shorn sheep back to the summer pasture, and they would start all over again the next day.

At noon, tata and Luba walked over to the side of the corral where they had left the lunch in the shade. Nicu finished his sheep, rolled and tied the fleece in a neat bundle, and sat down with them in a patch of grass that still felt cool against his fingers. I can't eat, he thought. His legs were so tired he wanted to lie down and not get up again that day. He couldn't do that. Tata wouldn't do that. Tata handed them food. Brown bread. Cold mamaliga with butter. Cold lamb. He didn't want to eat lamb today. He tried a little bread. It was good, and he drank some water to wash it down. He found he was very thirsty. He tried the mamaliga, cool and grainy against his tongue, and suddenly he was hungrier than he could ever remember being, and he ate greedily, even the lamb, astonished at how good it tasted. He knew he couldn't stop until he was more than full. Afterwards he was a bit sick, but he had been so hungry. They rested. Luba was helping by bringing sheep from the pasture for them to shear, and rolling and tying the finished fleece. She had a scarf tied around her hair and wore a man's shirt and overalls.

It was time to go back to work, but he was sleepy from the big meal, and the sun seemed hotter than before. Luba brought him a spindly looking ewe. This one was really dirty, the wool wouldn't be worth much. She must have been sick, the wool was so uneven. Didn't Chisholm know how to look after sick animals? He worked slowly, disgusted by the scrawny body, the dirty wool. He had reached the belly when something exploded in the wool, shooting streams of blood into the wool, spraying warm drops on his wrist. His stomach heaved. Christ! A tick. He *would* have to hit it. He worked fast now. The fleece wouldn't be worth anything. He held his belly rigid as he rolled and tied the fleece, then cleaned his wrist on some dry grass.

Luba was ready with the next one. He sighed. He could already feel the round warm shape against his body, the heat and texture seeping into his skin. His arms had always held sheep, would always hold them. They would be shearing here for a whole week, morning till dark. Then their own flock. Dumnezeu!

This one bleated and looked scared. For God's sake, I'm not going to hurt you, he thought. The runty ewe panted in the heat, her ribcage rapidly lifting, falling. Nicu threw down the shears. He was tired of doing things to sheep that they didn't want, holding their warm compact bodies, tired of the stupid sheep eyes.

Too bad, it had to be done. Sheep don't have anything to say about it, their eyes don't have expressions, not like human eyes. He wanted to strike the ewe, kick her. When she tried to run from him, he grabbed one back foot, and threw her easily to the ground. She tried to get up, and he dumped her to her rump, legs stretched forward, the position for shearing. He held her very tight between his knees, his body tense and hard. The ewe struggled, and he tightened his hold. Then she went limp, leaving him holding tight to a slack soft body. He felt a lightness in his belly and took deep breaths to keep his food from coming up, as he let the ewe fall in a heap on the ground. "Shit!" he cried, and walked unsteadily to the fence and the covered sealer of water.

It was almost empty. Nicu drained the last of it and looked around for Luba, who was also supposed to bring water. She must be off taking a leak somewhere. He was really thirsty now. Tata was at the far end of the corral, looking at a sick ewe. Nicu sat down for a moment on a rock, flexing his hands, growing stiff now from the constant grip on the shears. He wiped sweat from his face with his shirt sleeve. Damn! where was Luba? He was really thirsty.

After a few minutes, Nicu opened the gate to the corral and chased back the scared ewe. Then he cut out another and shooed and pushed it into the corral. He picked up the shears again, adjusting his grip to try to ease the aching fingers. He soon forgot his thirst, forgot everything except holding sheep and cutting away their wool. Then Luba was there, bringing another ewe, rolling the finished fleece. He felt fresher, felt pride in the work again. There was that moment when, if you did it right, the sheep could just get up and walk away from its fleece, and the fleece was so neat and whole you could bend and roll it up into a smooth bundle. Then it was like you had a new sheep, "just as nice as if you carved it out of butter," tata had said.

Nicu saw something move beside him. He turned, expecting Luba, and saw a girl watching him. Tall and dark-haired, she wore a pink and white gingham dress and pink ribbons in her long wavy hair. Margaret Chisholm. She held a sealer of water out to him; she had seen it was empty and refilled it. He hadn't even seen her watching. He'd thought she and her mother would keep to the house while the hired help were doing their work. He reached out and took the sealer. He was conscious of his bare arms, the smell of his body bathed in sweat. Well, too bad, that was what happened when a man worked. He was not ashamed.

"I noticed you were out of water," Margaret was saying, "so I brought some from our well. To save your sister having to go for it." Her face looked quite friendly, and this suggested a startling thought. Perhaps she was not like her father.

"Thank you, that was kind thing. Very hot sun," he said looking up at it. He didn't know what to say next. It would be only polite to drink some of the water.

"Try some," she suggested, "it's nice and cold, from a deep spring." She smiled, and Nicu thought how pleasant her brown eyes were. He opened the jar and tipped it to his lips, swallowing the icy water, feeling her eyes on him. All his thirst came back, and he gulped the water till his throat ached. He had to wait until he could bear to drink more.

He drank again until he couldn't bear the cold. It was good water, pure and sweet, not like the iron-tasting well water at home. When he lowered the jar, he was out of breath, the ache in his throat almost stunning. She was smiling again, seemed pleased that he'd enjoyed the water. This time it was easy to smile back, feeling the pulsing in his throat and the hot sun sparkling on everything.

He saw the paleness of her skin, her clean pink dress, and the contrast of his grimy work clothes, the heat in his armpits and crotch, the dark tan of his skin. The Chisholm women protected their skin from the sun. His own sister and mother worked outside in the sun, felt no shame at their sun-browned skin. But Margaret was smiling, did not feel he was not as good as she was.

"Thank you, Margaret Chisholm," he said, "Water very good."

Just then they heard Luba coming with another sheep. Margaret climbed over the corral fence, and Nicu screwed the top on the sealer and put it to rest by the fence. He went back to work with new strength, working very hard so Luba wouldn't notice anything, although he wasn't sure what there was to notice. When he looked up again, Margaret was gone, but he felt different. There was warmth in his belly. She did not think he was dirty, and he thought maybe she liked him. Yes, he was pretty sure Margaret Chisholm liked him. Late in the afternoon, when he stopped for more of the water, it was no longer cold, but the good taste was still there. When he began shearing again, he noticed he was working on the ewe that had been afraid. This time he was patient, handling her very gently, talking to her. He tried to show her she wouldn't be hurt. He worked as quickly as he could, and when he finished, took a few moments to stroke her and talk to her. This time it was much better. She would be all right.

August 1913

Chapter
NINE

The dirt felt warm and soft under her feet; it settled in the lines of her skin, worked its way under toenails. It was good to feel the earth warm again, the sun warming you right through.

Luba pulled at a tall weed with long flat leaves and yellow flowers like a pale dandelion. The tough roots held, the broken stem oozing a milky sap. Then she put out her tongue and tasted. It was strong and sharp, reminding her of the slightly sour smell of wild flowers. How did the earth make plants with so many tastes? Was the strong juice the taste of the earth? She shivered at the bitterness lingering in her mouth and went to the garden fence where tall grass grew. She plucked several stalks, carefully so that they separated from their sheaths, leaving the pale green tips. She chewed on these, their fresh sweetness mingling with the bitterness from the milky juice.

She went back to her row of cabbages, pull-

ing the weeds between them. The bending made
her back ache, that and her monthly bleeding. It
came oftener now, almost every month, and she
could tell when it was coming, by the ache in her
back, the pain and tingling in her breasts.

She didn't know the names of the weeds, but
each was a picture she remembered. The one
with milky sap was called "milkweed," although
there were also other plants called by that name.
She pulled at a weed, and it broke off near the
ground. Dandelions and milkweeds did that if
you weren't careful, then you had to dig them out
with your fingers. She hated most the low spreading weeds. You had to capture all the winding
tendrils and pull gently, or the stems broke away
in your hand, leaving the root to grow again.
And you had to carry the weeds away; if you left
them lying on the ground, some would root and
grow again. It felt good to pull the whole weed
out, without breaking it. You could feel in your
fingers how the root tried to hold on, but you
could ease it out. Except every now and then a
root was stronger, and there you were again with
the stalk in your hand.

She straightened up a moment to ease her
back, looked out across the big garden. She suddenly knew she could never get all the weeds. By
the time you reached the end, they had grown
back again where you started. It was too much
for one person. Luba frowned. Mama seemed so

tired these days, her feet and ankles swollen, her face pale and puffy. It was at least another month before the baby would be born, but already most of the housework and chores fell on Luba's shoulders.

Luba looked up at the house, sun hot on her back. Soon she should stop and make something to eat. Probably some pea soup, and there was some nice covasut to eat with it. And green onions, that would taste good. There was a movement at one of the upstairs windows, in mama and tata's room. Then mama's white face at the window. Mama calling something, calling her name.

The babies were too small; Luba didn't see how they could live. Any of the little heads would fit neatly in her palm. The three babies — all girls — had tiny wrinkled red bodies, and amazingly thick black hair plastered to their heads with the creamy yellow stuff that covered them. Her sisters. She couldn't believe it. They weren't breathing right. She wanted to call tata, but mama said no, don't go. Stay here with me.

At the window a fly buzzed behind the bottle-green blind that kept out light but not the heavy heat that filled the room. The white lace curtain was still. Luba thought about bathing the babies in a basin of warm water from the reservoir. No, she thought, better to wait, it wasn't safe to pick up these babies. Their colour didn't look right. She wished tata would come in from the pasture. She couldn't go to find him, couldn't leave mama. Nicu was in the corral near the barn, but if she called him, mama would hear. If only he'd come to the house for something. Something else was bothering her. Each of the babies cried as it was born, but now all three slept, their only movement a shallow breathing. She was afraid they would die and she wouldn't know it.

Mama was awake again. She cried out in pain, her eyes looking into Luba's. Another baby was coming! No, it couldn't be! Nobody had four babies at once. Mama struggled to raise her back against the metal bedstead; Luba stood behind the bed and helped her. She wet a flannel cloth and wiped mama's twisted face. "Shall I send Nicu to get tata?" she asked.

"No! Don't call him," she gasped. "Stay here with me."

This baby took no time at all. It was a boy, smaller than the others. His body looked thin and weak, and his skin was streaked with blood and the creamy stuff. Only the tiny eyelashes fluttered. Mama moaned. Already she was sinking back into sleep. Luba wet the flannel and cleaned away some of the blood.

Delicately, she stroked the small chest, then turned the baby sideways and stroked his back with warm soft hands. Come on, her mind said to him, try — try to breathe. The baby opened his eyes for a moment and seemed to look at her. He began to cry, a tiny distant voice. He felt cool, even in the hot room. She wrapped him in a soft diaper. Mama was asleep, her breath coming in jagged gasps, her fingers moving and twisting against the sheets, soft brown knots. Luba was afraid to cut the cord. She was afraid the baby was dying.

Luba edged towards the door, watching to see if mama would notice. She opened the door and stepped into the hall, closing the door behind her. She ran downstairs and out the kitchen door. She had to find Nicu. He was in the small pasture beside the barn. She willed him to look up, so she could beckon. Just then he did look up and saw her, waving wildly at him. He came running to the house.

"Go to the pasture and bring tata. Hurry!" He looked at her face, and without a word, he turned and ran. Luba went back to the room.

The babies lay in a row beside mama. Three sisters and a brother. Gently she stroked their chests, as if this might ease breath into them, and spoke soothingly as mama did with babies. But she soon stopped, because they didn't seem to hear her.

The three girl babies still slept, hardly breathing at all, but the boy cried softly. His arm moved and he brought a tiny fist to his mouth.

Luba picked him up and went on stroking his
chest. Then he opened his eyes, seemed to look
right at her. "He knows me," she thought, but
knew it couldn't be true. There was a choking
sound in his throat, then a rattling cough. She
patted his back. "Come on!" she begged, "come
on!" The baby coughed until the mucus in his
throat was loosened. Then he began to cry again,
and Luba thought his voice was growing
stronger.

   it is too much, Stefan, i told you we should
never have come here   better to have stayed in
the old land, where we knew the ways   we will
never belong here, *never*

   what is that buzzing sound?   i must find out,
i must ask Luba

   this is not a good place for us   even the people here call it bad lands   the badlands   there
isn't enough grass here for the sheep, there's never
enough water, and it's too hot in summer   in the
old land i remember trees, and the green hills of
Ramoiesti   it is never green like that here, Stefan, only a pale colour in spring

   Stefan, listen to me, this is not a good country
for us   can you not see?

   they kill my boy   i don't understand how
that could happen   we have talked of this many
times, but it is no more clear to me than it was

i don't understand, i tell you *why did you do nothing?*

i know, draguts, it was not your fault, what could you do? they ran away and no one would help us we did not know their language i will *not* learn to speak it

Stefan, my legs feel like they will never move again can you not do something about that buzzing i hear?

in the old land there was more music, everyone could make music you remember my brother Gigel he could play the pipes of pan so the sheep danced on the mountain

and then the storms when we sailed on the ship some days the wind blew so hard they wouldn't let us up on deck trapped in the heaving belly of the ship with no fresh air, people sick everywhere, they could not help it i would not be sick, i would not let it happen, and yet the smell alone would turn your stomach i would close my eyes and scream and scream in my mind, but on the outside i kept quiet so the children would not be afraid sometimes they clung to our legs in fear

i never thought we would get here alive i thought we'd be caught forever on the sea, great waves tossing us about in my mind i could see our village, but i knew we could never get back across all that water Canada was nothing, i believed we would never see that either we just hung there while the sea tried to drown us

what's that? that buzzing sound! can't you do something? where is Luba? i told her not to leave me she must help me with the babies

it is so *hot*, Stefan

on the boat there was a child sick in his throat, like Trian the night before we saw land again, the sea was so rough, no one could hold their food i was finally sick too why do bad things always come together like that?

just a little boy, about three years old his mother still nursed him she was from our country, Zoica she was called she was just a girl, very poor she wore a dull grey dress, like the sparrows here in winter, but her shawl was beautiful, embroidered all over the child cried from the pain in his throat, his forehead burning to the touch all night, he raved in his sleep, calling for his friends i said she should sleep, i would watch him, but she wouldn't go her husband was already in Canada, she was going on the boat to meet him she wouldn't sleep the child kept calling: "Dinu, Dinu, come and see the little flute I've got Dinu, come and see, come and see!" his eyes were very bright, but he didn't see us, just the children back in their village

i was sorry for her, but i was glad it was not my boy she tried to cool him with wet cloths, but it was not enough the air was so filthy and hot after a while i fell asleep and woke again just before dawn   the child was quiet now, i could see he was dying   i never saw that before, but i knew   his life seemed to flow out of his body, there was nothing that would stop it   Zoica wouldn't let go of him   she held him and rocked him, her cheeks red and fevered too   she was going to meet her husband   i didn't want to look in her eyes

it is so hot   i wish Luba would bring me a little water

do you remember my tata's house, Stefan, on the hill in Ramoiesti, overlooking the village? our house was nearest to the church   mama and i would sit on the balcony in the shade of the poplar trees, spinning   such a fine balcony, the railings carved in pretty shapes   there i sat to make my wedding clothes   that was all the work i had then, my tata wanted me to have good things

the people on the ship lost one of our boxes, Stefan   bed linens and woven rugs my sister made us   the skirt and blouse with flowers embroidered all over that i wore for our wedding   you said how fine i looked in them   and how we feasted—the roasted lamb, sweet wine, tsuica smooth and burning in the throat

that night, our first time together   our candle burning on the table, your face gentle in the light

i could feel the breeze from the window when you came to me, draguts, i was not afraid

you held me in your arms, touched my breasts

under my nightdress i was not ashamed when you lifted away my nightdress, your skin warm and sweet against me you stroked my hips i was trembling, draguts, but i was not afraid

i was not afraid when you came into me i didn't know anything then the other girls said it would hurt, but you never hurt me i thought, good, this is what it means to be man and woman, and it was as if i had always known

afterwards we saw that our candle had burned down we blew it out and lay together in the dark

but Stefan, my wedding clothes are lost you tell me it doesn't matter, we will get other things

where will i find such things again, there is nothing like them here in Canada these people laugh at the dress of our country, but the clothes here are so ugly i cannot feel beautiful in these clothes and the sheets, there is nothing here like them, my sister Nadia embroidered them with flowers and birds

me tu! I have been wanting to speak to you about Nicu he will marry the Chisholm girl you see how he looks when he speaks of her i know that look he will marry her, Stefan, and go away and speak English he says he will be called Nick from now on, the English way and what is wrong with our way?

she is very pretty like a little bird he is taken by her soft white skin, her silky hair their

children will be weak and pale, like skim milk
he will go away and speak English, and they will
eat white bread   i will never see my grand-
children   they will be ashamed of me   perhaps
you should speak to him, Stefan   but it's no
use   they will go to school together, it's too late

Trian was a good boy   our first child in this
country   i nursed him for more than a year   so
sweet tempered it was a pleasure to hold him
when i was a little girl, Nadia and i had a picture of Jesus as a little baby   Trian was like that
picture, like the little baby Jesus

Stefan, i can't put it from my mind   when i
touched him, his forehead was still warm, but
the life was gone from him   *but he was still
warm*   couldn't we have done something even
then to save him?

i have asked myself if it happened because we
do not keep the old religion   i know you don't
like me to say so, but this may be the reason we
have troubles   Trian was not baptized   i have
tried to be a good woman, but i think we have
done wrong

this now is too much, Stefan   four babies at
once   it is not *right*, Stefan, only animals have so
many

we are to blame, Stefan, we should never
have come here   this is not a good place for us
i am ashamed   i will not let you see them   i will
make Luba tell you that the baby died   i will

bury them, i will not let you see them

   each time, i thought, thank God it's finished
i didn't want to believe there could be more
they were so small, they came quicker than other
babies   but i had to help them more, they had so
little strength of their own   they hurt me inside

   i am very tired, Stefan, my legs have gone
dead   soon my breasts will be full, but my milk
will all dry up   i think there is a fly buzzing in
this room, i wish that someone would kill it

   how i long for the cool breeze from the mountains   this country is too hot in summer   everything dries up   i have watched the hills when
the heat waves roll across the badlands and the
earth shimmers as if it was on fire   fire eating up
the grass and the air   i am weary of this place
and now these babies   what does it mean?   we
have done wrong, Stefan

Chapter
TEN

The three little girls died the day they were born, before Stefan could reach the house. Then it seemed as if the boy would die too. But he hadn't died, had gained strength with each passing day. Gheorghe, whom Stefan had insisted on calling after his brother who died in the old country, was a strangely quiet baby. It was almost as if he knew his mother hadn't wanted him. Oh, she was gentle when she nursed him, but Stefan had often seen a blank look in her eyes as she gazed at the baby. And then a look of guilt, because she knew that she didn't feel what a mother should feel.

Stefan buried the babies on the hillside behind the house, beside the grave of Trian. He knew now that this was illegal, but he did not care. It was what Sofie wanted, and it was what he wanted.

Sofie wanted it partly because she was ashamed. No one must ever know. It was unnatural to have four babies at once, she said. Stefan didn't believe that, but some of her horror infected him. Four at once, he thought, and only one living.

Sofie said it was a punishment from God. Stefan tried to reason with her. If having four babies was a punishment in itself, why would God then take them away? What was the use of a punishment if it was taken away as soon as you knew about it? She told him not to be so stupid. Both things were punishments — the unnatural birth and the deaths.

He and Luba had washed the babies, both of them silent and amazed at the sight. He tried to comfort Luba. The babies were too small to live, he told her, and she nodded. But when Sofie spoke of punishment, he saw the fear in Luba's eyes.

It was time now for Luba and Nicu to get ready to go to school. Luba was fifteen years old and Nicu was sixteen, and they had never been to school, because there had never been enough children at Fair View to start one. Stefan had tried to teach them the little he knew about reading, but it had never seemed to mean much to Luba and Nicu. But he remembered how little he had been able to do after Trian's death, and he didn't want his children to be as ignorant as he was.

And now Sofie had decided she didn't want

them to go after all. Almost every day they had what seemed like the same argument, in slightly different words. They were having it again today.

"Stefan," Sofie said, "I don't want them to go. Not this year."

"But it's important. They have to learn. In this country everything is done by papers. A paper to come into the country, a paper to own land, a paper for a child when it is born. The children must know how to read."

"But—"

"And if they don't go this year, you'll say they're too old," he continued.

"I know what you're saying, draguts," Sofie said. "But, please, let's not send them. They will go away soon enough and learn English and marry English people."

"Oh, is that it? They'll marry English people if they go to school."

"Well," she said, "they might."

"We already know who Luba's going to marry," he said. "We've always known she'd marry Kosma and Nina's Paia."

"Oh, Luba, of course. I'm not worried about Luba."

"Well, what then?"

"Stefan, you aren't listening to me. I won't have all my children go away from me."

"You'll still have Gheorghe."

Sofie frowned. "I've been meaning to speak to you about him. Gheorghe must be baptized."

"No, Sofie, I will not allow it," he said.

And they were into it again. The church. The priest. God. Punishment. Stefan tried to keep calm.

"The church tells us every child must be baptized," Sofie said.

"I don't believe everything the church tells me," he said.

"Luba and Nicu are baptized," she pointed out.

"That was before. I have nothing to do with such things now."

Sofie spoke very softly. "They say a child must be baptized to go to heaven."

Somehow the idea of heaven enraged him. "Heaven? Where is that? Can you show me heaven?"

"You know I cannot," she said sadly. "I cannot show you heaven or hell. And yet there may be such a place as hell."

"Hell is a story," he said, "made up by priests to scare us. Show me in the Bible where it says there is such a place."

"You know I can't read. But the priests have more knowledge than we do." She was almost pleading with him.

"Yes!" he was angry now, "and how do they use that knowledge? To make us give them money for their churches and monasteries. I tell you I'm through with all that."

"I want Gheorghe to be baptized. Many nights I think about Trian, that he was not baptized. Stefan, his soul may not be in heaven."

"Listen, Sofie, don't believe such things. When someone dies, he goes into the ground. His body and soul are at peace."

"How can you be sure?"

"I spend many hours reading the Bible. I don't need any priest to help me read the Bible."

"But Stefan," she said, "it was the priest who taught you to read."

"That rotten bastard! I wish there was a hell, it would be too good for him. He said Mihail Gheorghe killed himself. He wouldn't bury him!"

"Stefan, don't talk so! You don't know what happened that night."

"My brother loved life, Sofie. Even when that devil of a boyar hounded him for his rents. He would never have killed himself."

"Every man has sins, Stefan."

"I tell you," he said, "I don't believe in a God that tortures people. I have thought about this a long time. I can't see any sense in it."

"Maybe it's not for us to say. The priest—"

"The priest! The priest! Do you not see I want nothing to do with any priest! My brother lies outside the churchyard!"

"But Stefan—"

"Enough! I take the blame. If our child is in hell, he will see his uncle there, and in time, his father. But there will be no priests here!"

"I am the mother. Does that mean nothing?"

"I can't help how I think."

"Nor can I," she said. "Did you ever think of that? You want Luba and Nicu to go to school. I want Gheorghe baptized like the others. You don't have to be there. Don't you see? If my little one is baptized, I won't be so afraid to let the others go?"

She was trying hard to sound reasonable, but it only seemed to enrage him further. "Now we're haggling over our children's souls?"

"I don't like to be afraid, Stefan."

"All right, I'll get the goddamn priest. It means nothing. Only a sprinkling of water and a few words. I could as soon do it myself. But I'll get the priest."

"Stefan—"

"I'll get the goddamn priest!"

Chapter
ELEVEN

Nicu balanced carefully to avoid spilling the milk in the shiny tin pails he carried. Behind him the clear blue light of the sky shaded to orange. At the house, Luba came to the door and took the pails from him.

Turning away, he walked up the hill behind the house, the light around him like a golden fog warming his arms, the stones, and the blades of grass. About halfway up, he sat down on a long flat boulder with a hollow in the centre, grey rock covered with fine veins and speckles of black, its sides crusted with lichens, rusty-red like dried blood. Tata said the lichens were alive. It was Nicu's favourite watching place.

The day had been hot, but now a cool breeze brushed his face and arms, his sweaty hair. He seemed to sweat more now than when he was a child. The smell on his skin was stronger, and in the hair of his armpits and crotch. He liked the smell, liked to touch his testicles, then smell the odour on his fingers.

He looked across the long lines of hills. Everything still looked sharp and clear in the fading light, no clouds anywhere, just the band of orange in the west. There, on the plain, he saw Coteau through a haze of light striking dust in the air. To the northeast, he saw Chisholm's house, heavy grey-brown stone touched by the slanting light. He thought of Margaret Chisholm in her pink gingham dress, getting ready for school in that house. He would see her tomorrow, because tomorrow he was going to school. He decided to heat some water from the rain barrel and have a bath after everyone was in bed. It would be nice to wash in the soft water, lathering his slippery skin, the hair of his armpits and crotch, settling into the warm water to rinse the suds away.

About half a mile to the south and west was a ridge of hills almost as high as the place where Nicu sat. As he watched the sky, he saw something move along the side of this ridge, dark and blurry. Then figures moved along the top of the ridge, and he saw them clearly against the light. Nicu felt a tightening in his belly. It was a band of horses. Wild horses, because there were about twenty, and nobody around here had twenty horses.

They ran lightly along the ridge, as if for pleasure, not away from anything, driven by a dark stallion. Nicu was afraid to move, even though

they were not looking his way. He wanted to go
tell Luba and mama and tata, so they would all
see. He started slowly to his feet, keeping his eye
on the horses. He was sure they couldn't see him,
but just then the stallion cocked his head, turned
the herd down the other side of the ridge. Nicu
stared at the place where they'd been running.

He looked down at the yard, saw tata moving slowly back from the barn, seeming to float
through the golden light that hung over the yard.
Nicu beckoned, but tata wouldn't look up. He
looked again towards the sun, and lost his focus;
the ridge of hills seemed to wave in front of his
eyes.

Nicu turned down the hill, away from the
house, into a long coulee. Hidden in the coulee,
he began to run, working his way towards the
place where the horses had disappeared. There
was a clump of stunted poplar and willow on the
other side of the ridge; the horses might be there.
He kept downwind of the clump of trees, his
body low in the coulees.

Nicu reached the hill that overlooked the
trees, and walked up the long slow sweep of it.
Near the top, he sank to his knees and crawled,
the hill above him a grassy curve that almost
filled the sky. At the top, he moved slowly on his
belly, the breeze cool now on his face. He saw the
clump of trees. They were there, cropping the
thick grass in the coulee. The mares moved easily

through grass and wolf willow, but the stallion kept pacing nervously around them. He watched always for any movement, watched the foals to make sure none strayed.

There was brush growing up the side of Nicu's hill. On his belly, he inched towards it, feeling the warm earth, breathing sage and wolf willow. The horses were only about a hundred yards away now, and he could see them clearly. A pair of magpies circled above their nest in the tallest poplar. The stallion was small and slender, a dark bay, like damp rich earth. Only his mane and tail were light, the colour of dry fall grasses. The mares were grey or white, except for a small black mare with a white blaze on her forehead. The foals were many colours from light grey to dark brown; some pintos, some solid colours. These horses looked rougher and shaggier than tame horses, but they had the light frame of saddle horses.

The stallion moved lightly around the herd, nodding and whinnying, running in a rough pattern of tightening circles, rounding them up for the night. As he passed the black mare, he reared as if to mount her, a paler shadow against her black body, then let one leg graze her flank as his feet sank slowly to the ground. She didn't move.

A pinto colt had strayed from its mother, and now wandered towards the hill where Nicu lay in the brush. The stallion saw and walked lazily after him, not making a sound. The colt grazed along the hill, unaware. Then the stallion broke into an easy gallop. Nicu felt his heart race as the earth-coloured horse moved closer and closer; he could see the muscles moving in the arched neck, almost feel the hoof-beats against the ground.

The colt whirled in the air, whinnying in terror, as the stallion nipped him hard on the flank. The stallion charged at the colt, and it galloped back to its mother in the shelter of the trees.

Now that he was up on the hill, the stallion decided to look around. Nicu could hear the dry swishing sounds of the horse's legs against the grass. It was darker now, and Nicu was well hidden in the brush, but the horse stood clearly outlined against the sky. Nicu lay frozen, almost afraid now, but still wanting to see. The horse paced around in the grass, scanned the tops of ridges, first to the north, then around in a wide circle, but never down at the place where Nicu lay. He kept moving up the hill, closer and closer. Christ, Nicu thought, he's going to walk right over me. He could see the eye of the horse now, the rough untrimmed hooves. He stared at the feet, rising toward him. The horse stopped.

The bay stallion saw him now, and Nicu forced himself to meet its eye. The horse just stood watching. Nicu couldn't move. The horse could kill him, trample him, if it wanted to. He didn't know if it knew that. It must, he was such a small creature lying on his belly in the brush. Like a snake, he thought. He wondered if he could move in time if the horse reared. He tried to tense his muscles to roll out of the way. But the horse didn't move, just looked at him.

There seemed to be no sounds around him now. He felt the sweat on his body, running down his armpit and soaking into his shirt. He could smell the sweat, and now the horse must smell it. The horse tensed slightly, as if preparing to attack or run, but still didn't move. Nicu stared at the large eyes of the horse. It was the first time he had ever really looked at a horse's eye, and he wondered now how he could have taken for granted something so alive, so different from human beings.

He was afraid now. The horse must know it could kill him, that people were its enemy. The stallion took a step forward. Nicu felt his chest would burst as he lay there, his belly twisting into a knot, hardly daring to breathe. Now, he thought, now he's going to come, and he stared at the horse as hard as he could, sucked a slow trickle of air into his lungs against the hard pressure of his tensed belly. Against the pressure of the earth. He kept his eyes frozen to the stallion's.

The horse snorted. Nicu felt the shock of the noise in his whole body, felt the horse's hot breath on his face. Then it reared in the air, hooves slicing the air above his head. I'm dead, he thought, but the horse turned in the air, twisted its body away from him, and galloped easily down the slope, whinnying to the mares. As the horse turned, Nicu saw the flank, dull brown in the dying light, a circle with the letter "R" in it burned into the hide. Nicu knew what it meant; it was the brand of the Rowland ranch, the biggest ranch in the south country.

The stallion never looked back. He overtook the herd and began to move them away, pushing the foals to go faster. In a moment, they were fading into the dark, falling away from his sight over the next ridge, as if the pools of dark air had whisked them away. Only their whinnies came back on the cool air.

Nicu felt the breath go out of him in a rush, and he was gasping for air. His throat hurt, and there was an emptiness in his belly as he watched the place where the horses had vanished into the dark. As he sucked the air into his lungs he was crying, for himself and for the earth-coloured stallion. Now his body was cold, his clothing damp. He lay shivering on the hillside, and his crying became stilled against the cool dry grass. He knew he should go home, it was cold. He got up, his legs weak and shaking, and began walking under the bright light of the moon.

Chapter
TWELVE

The hard wood pressed against his knees, the desk was made for a child. Doamne! It must be nearly time to go home. His muscles were stiff from sitting so long, and he ached to stand and stretch them.

There wasn't enough air to breathe. The school had been closed up all summer, and the open windows hadn't cleared out the stuffy smell of varnish and dust. A breeze from the window reached him, and he smelled the sweet sage and grass. Already Nicu saw himself walking home across the hills, leaving the school behind. He thought of the dark stallion running free across the hills.

The desk was built for a child, and he was almost a man. He ran his fingers over the desk top. He didn't like the feel of the wood, stained dark so you couldn't see the grain through the thick varnish. It felt tacky against his fingers, as if it had never been cleaned from the years of sticky fingers. Someone had carved letters into the wood, and he traced these with his finger. He didn't know what the letters meant.

Tata said they were lucky to live near a school. This was Sweet Grass School, the oldest school in the badlands, except for the school in Coteau.

He couldn't remember ever being so hungry. It felt like the sides of his stomach were pressing together, trying to get something to work on. He saw himself walking, fast, over the hills. He was angry, he wanted to leave this school. He didn't understand anything. All day he'd watched the teacher writing on the big slate on the wall at the front of the room, and he hadn't learned a thing.

He was the biggest boy in the school. Except for James and John Chisholm, Margaret's brothers. They didn't want her to talk to him. She smiled at him once, but they didn't like it. The Chisholm boys didn't look like Margaret at all. They were sandy-haired and barrel-chested like their father and their faces already had a set, suspicious cast like his. John was the older one, about seventeen years old, but James was louder and stronger. They laughed when Nicu made mistakes in English.

Luba didn't seem to understand anything either. She was afraid to answer the teacher. Miss Scrimshaw had asked Luba what was her name. "I have fifteen year," she had answered. All the children laughed, and Nicu's face burned with shame. "I asked what is your name, what are you *called*?" the teacher said. Then Luba understood, and told the teacher her name. The Chisholm boys snickered, as if there was something wrong with the name.

He would have to get up soon, his back was getting so stiff. It *must* be nearly time. The teacher stood at the front of the room, leading the grade fours and fives in their reading. They would stand up and read in turn from a little book. It made no sense to him at all. Nicu's desk was at the very back of the room, along the windows. He stared out the window, at the hills outside, the little barn beside the school, the wooden toilets.

In the middle of the morning, the teacher let them go outside to play. For a moment he had thought it was lunch time, but no, not yet. It was called *re-cess*. That was when they found the toilets. He hadn't known there would be two, but he saw all the girls went to one place, all the boys to another.

At recess they played ball. On what looked like a big square worn into the grass, but was called a diamond. You tried to hit a ball with a big round stick called a bat. If you hit the ball, you ran around the diamond. The corners were called first base, second base, and third base, and you could stop at any one of them. If you made it back to where you started, then you were home. His first turn at bat, Nicu swung three times without hitting the ball. This meant he was out. A little girl had gone out before him, so he knew what it was, thank God. Knew enough to put the bat down and take the little girl's place in the field out past third base.

Then Margaret hit the ball over second base. Nicu was ashamed that she could do it and he couldn't. Then it was Luba's turn, and she also managed to hit the ball, but it only dribbled along the grass, and she was put out too. The tall red-haired girl who took the bat next patted Luba's arm and spoke to her. She was called Beryl Langford, and she didn't laugh at foreigners.

Then James Chisholm was up. Nicu watched the way he planted his feet, the way he held his arms and shoulders, as he made practice swings with the bat. Then the ball shot towards him, and James swung with all his force, hitting the ball far past the fielders. A little boy in denim overalls ran down the hill after it, while James ran all around the diamond. This was called a home run.

Finally it was Nicu's turn again, and this time he was sure he could do it. He saw that James Chisholm was throwing the ball to him, and frowned. James had changed places with another boy. He stood talking with his brother until the other children yelled at them to get going, then they both laughed, and James got ready to throw.

The first pitch was too high, but Nicu wanted to hit so badly that he swung wildly at it and missed. He got ready again, planting his feet and swinging the bat. James took his time getting ready to throw, then the ball was whizzing straight at Nicu's face, and he stepped back and half turned. The ball caught him hard on the shoulder. He fought to hold back tears of pain and anger. He wanted to rush right over and fight with James, but he couldn't.

"James!" Margaret was yelling. "You be careful!"

Nicu got ready to hit again, trying to forget the throbbing in his shoulder. This time the ball came fast, but it was right across the plate. He was ready, he hit it as hard as he could. There was a loud crack and pains shooting up in his arms. He had actually broken the bat. James had caught the weak hit and thrown it to first before Nicu could drop the shattered stub of the bat. And then the bell was ringing, calling them back to school, and he was so ashamed.

All the students were put in grades, according to how much they knew. Margaret and her brothers were in grade twelve, the highest grade. Her brothers must be two or three years older than her, why were they all in the same grade?

When it came time to put him and Luba into grades, Nicu could hardly look up. He knew nothing of the things that were taught here. Even the littlest children knew more. But the teacher just said they wouldn't decide right away. "We'll wait and see how you do." Maybe they could learn really fast. But how? He wanted to scream. How could he learn fast if he didn't even know what the teacher was talking about? He didn't want to look stupid in front of Margaret Chisholm. Better to quit.

Who needed to know these things anyway? He could do a man's work already. Maybe he couldn't do things with numbers, but he knew how many sheep they had, how many lambs. Why did he need to know those other things? His learning was in his hands, his learning was from tata.

Maica Domnolui, it must be nearly time to go home. He was so hungry his stomach was hurting, and he hadn't even done any work today. They'd had mamaliga and cold lamb for lunch, but that seemed like ages ago. The other children had stared at the mamaliga. *"Mush!"* one little girl had said and giggled. Christ, he didn't care what the teacher said, he was going to have to get up, he couldn't stand it a moment longer.

Then children were walking past his desk towards the door, moving all together as if someone had given them a signal. They were all talking at once. School was over! Luba looked at him hesitantly, afraid to get out of her desk. He got up, nodding at her to do the same. All his muscles felt stiff and shrunken, and he stretched them to make sure they would still work. They followed the other children out of the school while the teacher stood at the front of the room, wiping the writing off the big slate.

It felt so good to be in the moving air again, to feel his legs striding under him. He wanted to walk as fast as he could, to get home again almost before he could think about it. He had never thought about time before. Now he knew that a day is a very long time. Tata had bought a small clock from Coteau, so they would know the time to leave for school. It stood on the table in the living room, making a loud ticking noise.

When they walked into the kitchen, there was mama making supper as usual, and Gheorghe sleeping in his cradle. Nicu felt happy just seeing them. It seemed a very long time since he'd left in the morning. Mama looked worried, as if she expected that already they would be changed by the things they had learned. As if they had gone into a world where she could never follow. Tata was coming up from the barn. He came into the kitchen too, and smiled at them. He looked so nice standing there, that Nicu wanted to put his arms around Tata and hug him. But he better tell him right away.

"I'm not going to school any more, tata," he said, trying to speak firmly, like a man.

"Oh," said tata, "and why is this?" Luba just watched him. She was helping mama, who was frying the little pancakes spread with jam to eat after their cabbage rolls. Nicu could see the finished ones on a plate in the warming oven, and he longed to grab one and gulp it down.

"Because it is of no use to me," Nicu replied. "And I'm too far behind. Even the little children know more than I do." Everyone watched him.

"You are sure it is of no use to you?" tata asked.

"Yes, I'm sure. I can do a man's work already."

"No." Tata spoke very quietly. "You're wrong."

"But I can work!"

"In this country it is very important for people to read and write. That is how everything is done here."

"But tata—"

"Listen to me! Everything you do here, you must have a paper. A paper to come into this country, a paper to be born, a paper to get married. A paper to show who owns land, and who owns houses, and horses. If you cannot read papers, everyone will cheat you!" Tata did not say, you have to have a paper when someone dies, but Nicu remembered.

"But tata, they laugh at us! They laugh at how we talk."

Tata looked sad. "Listen. You know I won't force you. But I'll tell you something. I left the old country. In our old village there, no one knows how to read or write, or count things on paper. Only the priest. We have to pay the priest to help us."

"Then a man came to our village. In Canada, he says, all children can go to school. Me, I don't know. It's too late. But if you will just learn now, my children, then we will all know. Your children will know, and their children. Our family will never be ignorant again." Nicu could not speak. "I'm telling you, Nicu, a man who wants to take care of himself, he has to know how to read."

Nicu knew tata was remembering Trian. He had no answer.

"Luba," tata said, "you don't like school either?"

"No."

"But will you try for a little while?"

"Yes, tata, for a little while."

"And Nicu? You will try too?"

"All right," Nicu said. "I will try too."

December 1913

Chapter
THIRTEEN

Nicu was sitting at the round table, reading from his schoolbook. The others, Stefan and Sofie and Musca, sat around the table too, except for Luba, who sat in Sofie's rocking chair, rocking Gheorghe to sleep. Musca had finally come for a visit.

Ffffft! A thick paring, whorled and yellow as horn, sailed through the air and landed on the iron stove. Nicu paused for a moment. Sofie glared at Musca, who smiled and shrugged, as if to say, "Who am I to know the ways of toenail clippings?" It curled and sizzled on the stove. Musca went to work on the next toenail, gripping the heavy shears with the greatest care. Pishoarca! Sofie was thinking. Something will have to be done. Nicu began to read again.

The wind howled around the house and sent cold fingers into the room, but the belly of the iron stove was full of coal and kept the people warm. The day had been cold and clear. In the morning, Sofie and Luba had finished the Christmas baking. The quiet afternoon had been full of work too, even Musca had worked, sitting by Sofie all afternoon, carding wool for her to spin. In the late afternoon, the wind had started to blow from the northwest, and the men had herded the sheep into the shed and given them feed. By supper time, they could see nothing from the window but whirling snow, with no dividing line between sky and land.

Gheorghe was fast asleep. Luba placed him gently in the cradle. Nicu finished reading.

"That was very good, Nicu," Stefan said, and Nicu looked proud. Musca made a little face, as though reading was not all that fine a thing. Who needed it anyway? Sofie saw the look. Useless tit! she was thinking. One of us is going to be leaving here soon, and it's not going to be me.

"What was that story about?" Sofie asked.

"It was a poem, a story told with rhyming words."

"Yes, yes—rima, we have that in Romanian songs too. You remember 'Stoianiel.'"

"Stoianiel, Stoianiel," Musca wailed, "Draga mama: 'strugaliel': Dimineatsa—" the song told the story of a handsome young man with black eyes who was killed by a woman he was courting. It had a great many verses, and Musca knew them all.

"We all know the song, Florian," Sofie said

sharply. Stefan looked at her questioningly, but her eyes did not soften. We will have to leave him at Kosma and Nina's when we visit at Christmas, Stefan thought. Musca had come in November, too late to help Kosma with his harvest, when it got too cold to sleep in the stable where he worked in town.

Stefan remembered bringing him home in a wagon, a special trip to Regina for no other reason. Musca had sat huddled in a big woolen blanket because he had no winter coat. He'd had a sheepskin from the old country, but lost it by gambling the week before. Sofie is not going to like this, Stefan had thought. Musca had smelled like the stable. Even Stefan had been a little offended. Surely those fancy women would refuse to sleep with a man who smelled that bad.

Luba was reading something now from her reader, a story about a little girl and her father who were on a ship in a terrible storm. She read very slowly, and Sofie could understand some of the English. That's a very fine story, Sofie was thinking, that's just how it was on the boat coming here, the winds, the waves crashing against the boat. The wind howled outside, and for a moment it was like she was on the boat again...

Musca had not been in the house very long that day in November before Stefan noticed something going on in the kitchen. Sofie was sending the children to the well for pails of water, and heating them in the boiler on the stove. She brought soap, a towel, and clean clothes of Stefan's.

"Cousin Florian," she'd said (he wasn't exactly a cousin, but it sounded friendlier that way), "I will be very glad to wash those clothes for you. In the meantime, here is warm water for a bath. Afterwards you can put on these things of Stefan's until yours are washed." Musca had looked embarrassed, but there'd been no choice. He made Stefan promise not to let anyone come into the kitchen, and even then kept looking every which way as if he was afraid they would. Is this the man who sleeps with bought women? Stefan had wondered.

Musca had come out of the bath smelling very good. Sofie had made a strong infusion of herbs and added it to the bath — camomile and sage gathered from the prairie in summer — and Musca had smelled of that sage when he came out, wearing Stefan's pants and shirt, with the cuffs rolled way up, his thin wet hair plastered to his head, in rough windrows where he'd combed it with his fingers.

Stefan had had to fight with his face that wanted very much to laugh at this momaie, this scarecrow of a man. Luba had started to laugh, but she'd covered up and smiled at him: "You look very nice, Uncle Musca." A smile had brightened his face for a moment, then he'd looked sad, his eyes drooping on either side of his long curving nose because he'd seen they were all laughing at him. Then Sofie had put the clothes in clean soapy water. She'd boiled them and boiled them. She'd probably wished she could boil Musca too. Again she'd added sage to the clothes water to make it smell good. She'd made sure Musca was going to be one clean man, for a little while anyway.

Luba was reading slowly, slowly.

Today everybody had had a bath. It was Saturday, and Nicu and Luba were practising the things they'd learned in school. Musca was still cutting his toenails — he really knew how to draw it out, could make it last through ten people reading if he had to. Another hard yellowed paring flew across the room, just missing the heater. He'd show Sofie he knew a thing or two about looking after his body, without anybody having to tell him.

There was a soft thumping sound in the kitchen. Luba stopped reading for a moment, then went on. The others looked at each other, shrugged. Must be the wind. Probably a fantoma, Musca thought, glancing nervously at Stefan. The sound came again, a little louder. Musca rolled his eyes and Nicu and Stefan leaped up and ran to the kitchen. At the door, they held back a moment, then Nicu opened it and a fierce blast of wind blew snow in from the lean-to.

There was someone huddled on the floor, like a bundle of dark blankets. It was Margaret Chisholm.

"Please," she sobbed, "I can't go any further." Nicu and Stefan helped her to her feet, arranging one of her arms around each of their necks. A scarf whitened by frost slipped away from the lower half of her face. Her eyelashes and eyebrows were white too. Nicu kicked the door shut as they half carried her to the couch, set her gently down.

Everyone stared and held back a moment. Musca gaped, seeing her frosted brows. "This is Margaret Chisholm, mama," Nicu said in English, although they all knew who she was, except Musca. He relaxed. It was not a fantoma, but some girl that Nicu knew.

Sofie came to the girl, loosened her scarf and handed it to Luba, then gently eased away her heavy woolen coat. She looked at Margaret's bright red cheeks, touching a warm hand to the two icy points in their centres.

"Nicu, go upstairs and bring blankets to wrap around her," Sofie said. "Luba, take off her boots." Nicu sprinted up the stairs, as Luba fumbled with the buckles on Margaret's boots. Sofie rubbed the girl's hands, and she cried at the pains that came as warmth slowly flowed back into them.

Nicu came down the stairs with blankets, his

heart pounding hard. He saw them all bent over Margaret. He brought the blankets and wrapped them around her. For a moment she looked up at him.

"Nicu," tata suddenly remembered, "see if she has a horse."

"Yes," Margaret answered weakly, "but don't go out there." Nicu took his jacket and went into the porch again. He opened the outer door, and there was Margaret's horse, looking half dead, standing meekly in the freezing wind.

He knew he couldn't make it to the barn. But there was an old shed near the garden. He could make it there by feeling his way along the fence. Not very warm, but shelter. He came in to put on his heavy coat and boots. Margaret saw him.

"No!" she cried, "don't go out there, you'll get lost."

"Put him in the old shed by the garden," tata said. "Hold on to the garden fence." Nicu nodded, and went out. Margaret tried to sit up, but Stefan put his hand on her arm.

"It's all right," he said, "Nicu will come back. He will hold on to the fence." Margaret sank back against the couch.

Luba had got the boots off and was rubbing Margaret's feet. Margaret began to cry again, and Musca watched, making little clucking sounds of pity. Sofie went to the kitchen to make tea. Musca still held the scissors, sitting with his feet bare against the cold boards.

"What has happen to you, Margaret Chisholm?" Stefan asked. She looked expectantly at the door, and tried to stop crying to answer him. Just then Nicu came back in and she gave a little sigh of relief.

"I got lost," she said. "I was nearly here and somehow I went the wrong way."

"But where were you going on such bad night?"

Nicu had taken his sheepskin off and was listening to her. "Oh, I didn't go out tonight," she said. "I started early this afternoon and rode to Langfords' to take Beryl her Christmas present. The weather was fine then, there wasn't even a wind. It's just three miles from our place."

Sofie came back with a cup of hot tea and a very small glass. Musca stared with disbelief as she poured into the glass the last drops of his very last bottle of tsuica.

"Here, dragutsa," she held the glass to Margaret, "drink. You feel better." She put an arm behind Margaret's back for support. Margaret made a face at the brandy, but she swallowed it a little at a time, helped by sips of the hot tea. Musca just shook his head sadly, his throat making little swallowing movements as he watched her drink. She wasn't even enjoying it!

"But I don't understand," Stefan said, "how you come this way from Langfords'. You lost your way?"

"Not right away. I left Langfords' when there was still about an hour's light left. There was no sign of a storm. But by the time I got to the school, the storm was starting—"

Sofie clicked her tongue. "You maybe should stayed at school."

"I thought about it," Margaret said, "but I didn't like to stay there over night all by myself. So I decided to come this way, because it's through the coulees and more sheltered, and I thought if it got really bad, I could stop here if I had too—"

"Of course, of course, we very glad you come here," Stefan said, and Margaret smiled at him. Nicu smiled too, because Margaret was here in his house. "But what takes you so long?" Stefan went on. "The sun is down now for two hours."

"After I left the road, I got lost. I thought I was getting close to your house and that I'd better stop, but when I got over the last hill, where I thought the house would be, it wasn't there... so I thought I went down the wrong coulee and I tried to go back. But I couldn't really see anything by then, so I just kept on, trying to see something that would show where I was... I couldn't feel anything in my hands and feet... I just kind of gave up and let the horse go where he wanted and I wasn't really thinking any more." Margaret was getting very sleepy. "Then after a while a saw your light... and I knew if I could just get to the door—"

"Doamne!" Stefan said. "You had much danger."

"I didn't think I'd be able to make enough noise for you to hear me—" her eyes were closing.

Sofie came with a cup of soup. "No more talk now," she said, "drink, then you rest." She looked around at the family, everyone watching the Chisholm girl. "I think it's time we go to bed now," she said in Romanian, looking at Luba and Nicu, who started to get up. "Luba, help me make a bed here on the couch. Nicu, it's time you are going to bed," and this time her look included Musca, made him fidget in the chair where he still sat and stared. He hadn't said a word since the girl arrived. He gathered up his socks and started to put them on. An idea came to him, and he smiled.

"The little girl can use my blanket if she likes," he said in Romanian. Nicu scowled at him.

"That is all right, cousin Florian," Sofie said, "we have enough blankets. But tonight you will have to sleep with Nicu, so we can make our visitor a bed here on the couch."

"Sure, sure," Musca said in English, "iss fine me." He smiled at Margaret as if she must appreciate the sacrifice he was making. Nicu scowled. He didn't like Musca looking at

Margaret like that. And now he had to sleep with him. Oh well, at least today Musca had taken a bath.

Nicu waited until everyone was asleep, even Musca snoring lustily beside him. Then he slid out of bed and pulled his shirt and pants on over his long underwear. Very quietly, he crept down the stairs.

She lay wrapped in heavy blankets and a quilt, only her face and one hand sticking out of the covers, her breathing easy and regular. Nicu wished he could take the hand and put it back under the covers, but he was afraid of waking her. The room was still warm. Tata had put more coal on the fire before they went to bed.

It was so dark he could barely see her. He sat on a chair by the couch, a blanket wrapped around his shoulders. It was nice to sit and hear her breathing, to feel the warmth coming from her, making wider and wider circles in the room, like when you threw a stone in water and it rippled out around the place the stone landed. He wanted to slide under the covers beside her and hold her.

Margaret stirred as if she were dreaming. Her breathing came faster, and her mouth moved. Nicu watched, wanting to wake her from the dream so she wouldn't be afraid. He held a hand out towards her as if to say, don't worry, it's all right. Margaret groaned and turned in her sleep.

Her breath came in gasps, and she held her hand in front of her face as though to keep something back. He longed to wake her up. It's all right, you're safe, he tried to tell her in his mind.

Her body moved sharply and her eyes came wide open. She saw him there, stared hard at him in the darkness. Then she recognized him and smiled, and a wave of joy swept over his body. He wanted to hold her in his arms, but he just sat, smiling at her. She closed her eyes, and right away she was sleeping again, her face smooth and peaceful.

Nicu's feet were getting cold. He watched Margaret a little longer, and when she kept sleeping calmly, he went quietly back up the stairs to bed.

Lifting the corner of the covers, Nicu became aware of two shining black objects. They were attached to the head of Musca, and they were wide open.

"Going for a little walk, eh Nicu?" he whispered. "Getting up to take a leak, were you?"

Nicu climbed in beside him and settled down in the covers, turning his back to Musca. "Go to sleep," he said, "it is very late."

Nicu heard a big swallowing sound and then a little snicker. "That neighbour's daughter, she's a pretty fine little mare, esta?" Nicu's body stiffened; this Musca was going to have trouble with his teeth if he wasn't careful. Musca felt him tense and added innocently, "Yes, she seems to be a very fine person."

"Yes, she is a very fine person, all right," Nicu agreed. "Now do you mind if we go to sleep?" He turned over again and tried to burrow down into the covers.

"Sure, sure, let's go to sleep now," Musca agreed. "Still," he said, "I was just thinking how lucky the man will be who gets to ride a little filly like that. I sure wouldn't mind — aah — aaaahh — "

Nicu's hands were around Musca's skinny throat, squeezing, and he was shaking him, up and down, so his head rose a foot from the bed, then came thumping down again. Musca was making gurgling noises in his throat, the bed was heaving, and Nicu heard a movement in his parents' room. Musca pounded the mattress with one hand, but he couldn't get free. The coal black bulging eyes gleamed imploringly at Nicu, but he didn't let go.

"Listen, you old pile of cacat, don't you ever talk that way about her again," Nicu whispered. "Understand?" He stopped shaking Musca a moment to get an answer. Musca tried to nod, his eyes bulging wider and wider, his chest almost bursting. "Understand?" Yes, yes, Musca was nodding, and Nicu gradually eased his grip on Musca's throat. Musca kept nodding vigorously as he gasped for breath, showing eyes full of fear to

Nicu, so he wouldn't start choking and shaking him again.

Nicu balanced on all fours on the bed, his face glaring down at Musca. "Because if you ever talk like that again, you're going to be very sorry," Nicu said, and Musca again shook his head to show he would never do it again, and made soft little motions with his hands that said, "Of course I won't do it," and "don't hurt me, please, I'm only poor little Musca."

"Because if you do, and I find out, do you know what I'm going to do Musca Graba?" Musca shook his head, as if he couldn't possibly guess such a hard thing.

"Do you *know* what I'm going to *do*?" Nicu hissed.

"No, no, I don't know at all," Musca replied this time, to keep the question from coming back again.

"Then I'll tell you, since you are so poor at guessing. If you talk like that again, Musca Graba, I will bring the sharp knife tata uses to cut up the little lambs—" he paused and Musca looked up at him, trying to make his eyes show more fear "—and I'll cut away a very important part of the body of Musca Graba that he'd be very sorry to do without—"

Musca's eyes widened in real horror. "You wouldn't—" he started to say, but Nicu glared down at him:

"That he likes to use to please the women—"

"No," Musca gasped, "no—"

"Your tongue, stupid one. Your tongue." Musca's rigid body relaxed a little at this. "But that's nothing to what I'd do if I ever heard that you had so much as touched her, even on her arm, even the top of her head, even her boot when she has been walking in the stable. Then what I'd do would be much more terrible."

"Do you hear me, copil de tsatsa? Pishoarca! Do you hear?"

Again Musca nodded. "Yes, yes, I hear. Don't worry, I'd never think of touching her, I was just teasing you a little. Didn't you understand?"

"I understand that you are never to try to touch her as long as you live, or ever talk about her that way again." Musca just wagged his head to show he wouldn't. "And I hope you understand the same thing."

"I understand, cousin Nicu, I understand. Don't be so angry, I will never again—"

"And now," Nicu said, "I have decided that I don't want to sleep with such an old pishoarca tonight, because I might wake up and find the sheets wet and then I would get cold." He got up out of bed and picked up Musca's pillow and one of the blankets from the bed. He threw these in a corner as Musca watched with fascinated black eyes. Then Nicu grabbed the wiry little man by the front of his nightshirt and lifted him from the bed. Musca's body went limp. The crazy boy had just started to calm down and now he was getting violent again.

There was a soft thumping sound.

"But cousin, I will freeze down here, it is very cold—"

"I'm sorry, but you should have thought of that before you offended me."

"But cousin—"

"Good night, Musca Graba, I'm very sleepy now."

"Nicu... ?"

"Good night, Musca!"

Musca began to settle himself on the floor. He pulled on his old sweater over the nightshirt, and his socks and then folded the blanket in half and tried to burrow down inside it. He rubbed at his throat to ease the soreness.

Actually he didn't need to piss, but to tell the truth, the fear and excitement had given him an urge to shit. But it was twenty below and blizzarding and a long way to the shithouse. Besides, how could he go outside now, past the sleeping girl? Nicu would think he was trying to molest her. He would probably kill him. He tried to think of something else so the feeling would go away. Ah, the pretty young girl... but no, the fear came back. He would think of his girls in town, that was good.

Nicu found he was very sleepy now. He settled himself down on his stomach, stretching out his arms and legs in the spaces Musca had left. The bed felt very comfortable tonight. He was so sleepy. He pulled the covers up high around his ears to keep out the cold drafts. Ah, that was nice, and so much room in the bed. He thought of Margaret downstairs, safe and warm, no longer afraid of storms or bad dreams. No one could say bad words about her. He was sinking into a lovely soft sleep, so warm. Margaret liked him. Margaret was here, sleeping in their house. Sleep was settling on him like a blanket, soft and warm.

In the morning Nicu woke to faint grey light and the sound of snoring in his ear. Musca slept peacefully beside him, his breath warm against Nicu's neck, one arm flung across his shoulders.

Chapter
FOURTEEN

At dawn, Stefan rode over to the Chisholms'. Although the mother's reaction was pure joy and relief, Chisholm seemed less happy to find his daughter was alive than he was angry and suspicious to learn where she'd found shelter. But Mrs. Chisholm would not be cowed. She took Stefan's hand and shook it warmly, thanking him, and telling him to thank his wife and family too. Only then did Chisholm give his grudging thanks. Stefan offered to bring Margaret home later, but Chisholm said he'd send his sons with the sleigh and team.

By noon the Chisholm boys, John and James, were in the yard, their sleigh filled with blankets and buffalo robes. Although Sofie didn't think the girl was ready to move, she and Stefan helped Margaret out to the sleigh. Nicu brought her horse from the shed and handed him over to James, who tied the bridle to the back of the sleigh. Soon Margaret was warmly tucked into the sleigh and the little procession moved slowly out of the yard, Margaret turning to wave a red-mittened hand.

Stefan knew Chisholm was angry about the whole thing. If there had been any way to suggest that the Dominescus had kidnapped Margaret for ransom, he would have done it. It hurt his pride to accept hospitality from foreigners; it hurt him much more to owe them his daughter's life. The next day he sent his son John over with a side of beef. Such an ample gift might be said to discharge the obligation, even generously. Stefan tried not to accept; it wasn't necessary, they didn't want a reward, they were only helping. But John Chisholm said something strange: he said, "Both my father and my mother want you to have it." And Stefan said to himself, why not, it is no less than he owes me. Not because I took his daughter in, but because of the shearing. I'm too poor to be so proud. So he thanked John, and when he helped John bring the beef into the lean-to porch, Sofie didn't say a word. She didn't look happy, but she wasn't saying they should take it away either.

It wasn't until Luba and Nicu went back to school after Christmas that they understood how angry Chisholm really was. Margaret was not back at Sweet Grass School. He had sent her to board in town, to finish her last term at the Coteau high school. When Nicu came home that

day, there was a look on his face that told Stefan
that Nicu wouldn't be going to school much longer.

For a few weeks he said nothing about quitting. He worked hard at his reading and arithmetic, as if he were trying to squeeze all the learning he could out of the last few weeks of school. Luba worked hard too; there seemed to be a change in her, something he couldn't quite understand, although he thought he should be able to.

One night this mystery became clear. It was a Saturday again, bath day, and again there was a knock on the door. Only there was no storm this time, and everyone knew it couldn't be Margaret. They opened the door and there stood a tall dark-haired boy, holding a deerskin bag. Luba looked embarrassed, but Nicu got up at once and brought him in and introduced him. It was Lachance, a boy they knew from school. Lachance always spent a few weeks or months in school each winter, but this winter he had started to come regularly. Now the reason was clear.

Sofie and Stefan welcomed him and gave him coffee and placinta, while Luba looked self-conscious and said almost nothing. Lachance was tall and slender, with a strong beautiful face. He had bright blue eyes set above strong cheek bones, and a hawk-like curving nose that made him look almost like a Romanian. The idea that this person was here because of her seemed to be pressing on Luba like a weight; up till now she'd been treated as a child, and no one came calling on her.

Stefan asked Lachance what was in the deerskin bag. A look of quiet pride touched his face and he drew out a home-made fiddle and bow. Sofie asked if he would like to play for them, and Lachance played them jigs and reels. The tunes sounded strangely to the Romanians' ears, but they soon took pleasure in their dancing rhythms. Before long, Stefan was able to play along on the flute, and Musca, who was still with them, whirled around the room.

Now that the cat was out of the bag, something had to be done. It had always seemed clear to everyone that Luba would marry Paia. But if Paia was still going to have a chance with Luba, he'd have to do his courting now. So the day after Lachance's second visit, Stefan found it necessary to visit Kosma and Nina to get some advice from Kosma about the best treatment for a sick ewe. After all, it was always nice to be sure, even though, back in their old village, Stefan had always been considered the best man to look after sick animals. And Stefan also found it helpful to have Luba along with him, to visit Petrica, who had been sick with some kind of fever.

After this trip, no one was surprised when Paia was sent over by his parents with something for the Dominescus. Kosma had made too much sauerkraut that winter, it seemed, and they were sending a barrel over so it wouldn't go to waste; and Nina was taking the opportunity to send Sofie a quilt she'd been making for her. Stefan happened to ask Paia if he wanted to stay a few days, and Paia said he guessed he could.

The next few weeks were terrible for Luba. She seemed to move in a trance half the time, and she had a puzzled frown on her face whenever someone wasn't talking to her directly. She would stop in the middle of some chore as if she'd forgotten where she was. Or she'd stand making cabbage rolls, her hands doing the work, and her mind somewhere far away. She spent a lot of time making placinta, and she seemed to be playing a game with herself to see just how thin she could stretch the pastry without tearing it. But when either Paia or Lachance came, she was terribly quiet. Everything was being said in silence.

The two boys were so much alike. Both dark-skinned and dark-haired, with perfect white teeth. Both young and strong, and agile riders. And one was watching her with his soft brown eyes, and the other with bright blue eyes. She seemed to feel the physical presence of each like a weight upon her own body, and that was the trouble. She could feel so much for each of them.

Once both of them came on the same day. They were so alike physically that she started to think of them almost as twins. Tata had suggested music that night, and soon both of them were playing a jig, with her tata and her brother playing along with them. It was all too much, and she had to go upstairs where she'd set up her spinning wheel, and she sat and finished two skeins of fleece before they finally gave up and went home.

There was no apparent tension between the boys. They seemed to understand that they would have to be patient and wait for her answer. For one thing was clear to everyone, even Luba, that she couldn't have them both. Even though she might think of it at times, she knew she couldn't really do that. She couldn't have them both at once, that was ridiculous, and she couldn't have them one at a time either. Yet the more she saw of them, the more they mesmerized her with their lean young bodies, the more impossible it seemed to just give one of them up. She couldn't give up Paia. She had known him since they were little children in the old country. Mama and tata had always intended that she should marry Paia, and she had always agreed. But she didn't want to give up Lachance either. She liked his eyes and his slender brown fingers on the fiddle, and she felt glad that he wanted her. Why did she have to give one of them up? Why did she have to hurt someone? Why was it up to her? And yet no one else could decide.

And so it went on. No one pressed her, but it was understood that she must give an answer soon. Luba tried to think, and finally she came up with a few clear ideas. Paia, she thought, had a stronger claim because he had cared for her for such a long time; he would be losing more if she didn't choose him. And he was one of her people, spoke the same language, played the same music. But Lachance, she admitted to herself, was more attractive to her now. He was new, not someone she had known all her life, and he seemed so full of energy and passion, and it was all beaming itself towards her. But she told herself that maybe that was only because he was less familiar to her. It didn't mean she didn't feel as much for Paia.

Finally she thought of one thing that was decisive. Paia wanted to marry her and raise sheep, the same work tata did. If she married him, they would both live here in this same house with mama and tata, probably for many years. She wouldn't have to leave her family. She wouldn't have to leave little Gheorghe, and she felt almost like a mother to him. Paia would work with tata, helping with everything. But if she went with Lachance, he would take her away from her family. It would be a different life, a more unsettled life. Lachance would probably join his father, who worked winters for a rancher, and then in summer moved through the south country with a Metis sheep-shearing crew. His people spoke a different language, played different music.

It wasn't easy to tell Lachance. She wished she hadn't learned that you could feel this way about two people at once. She knew she would feel the gaze of his blue eyes for the rest of her life. For the rest of her life, a part of her would wonder where he was, what he was doing.

After Luba had chosen, Nicu seemed to come to a decision too. He had learned from Paia that men were being hired at the Rowland's brick yard in Coteau. Margaret was at school in Coteau. Everyone knew that she had sent him a letter, but he had never said a word of what was in it. Now Nicu told them he was going. He rode to town one day, and when he came back, he had the job. And a boarding place in town. And for all that either Sofie or Stefan could say, there was no budging him. Paia would be coming soon and then he could take Nicu's place helping tata. It took away Nicu's last remaining feeling of guilt about going. Paia was coming.

Within a week Lachance was gone too. He stopped going to school, and got a job as a hand on the Rowland ranch. And although it was Nicu everyone talked about, it was like they had lost another member of their family; one they hadn't known as well, but one who had a claim on them now, too.

May 1914

Chapter
FIFTEEN

The man watched as a figure on a horse climbed slowly up the road from Coteau, riding west, towards the hills of the Rowland ranch. He squatted on a grassy hummock, sucking at a hand-rolled cigarette; his bay mare grazed in the ditch. The rider looked up, and he could see curly brown hair under the grey felt hat. She raised her arm and waved.

There was a dip in the road and the girl slowly sank into it, then reappeared, closer and bigger. She was urging the horse to go faster, but it refused to do more than walk up the steep road. She shrugged and held her palms out in the sunny blue air, as if to say, what can I do? He could see her clothes now; she wore men's corduroy trousers, silvery grey like the felt hat, but her blouse was a woman's, of cream coloured cotton, with rows of vertical tucks edged in lace across the breast, and lace at the cuffs and collar. Mama was wrong when she said the English made no pretty clothing.

She pushed back her hat, which was held by a cord under her chin, and he saw her hair, braided and wound around her head, a fringe of loose curls framing her face. Into the braids she had woven ribbons that trailed out behind like streamers, crimson, muted and soft like the hat.

He got up to meet her, shaking the stiffness from his legs, taking a drag on the cigarette and flipping it to the road. She reined in her horse and waited for him. Their eyes met.

Margaret bent in the saddle, and Nicu reached up to her. Without turning, she lifted her leg backwards over the saddle, belly against the pommel, and slid down into his arms just as smooth as butter. He closed his eyes, feeling the silky touch of her blouse, her cheek, his hand running over the thick clump of braids warmed by the sun, the horse's warm hide against his shoulder. He pressed his face against her throat under her ear, to smell the clean sweet smell there.

They led their horses across the ditch and along the barbed wire fence to a gate where a trail cut across the prairie. They looked all around them, but there was no one in sight. Nicu opened the gate and Margaret walked the horses through. He closed it carefully after them, with a loop of wire over the fencepost.

"I ride up here yesterday," Nicu said. "Cattle are still in winter pasture, so there won't be anybody around. We can get to the valley easy." They mounted the horses. They were on Rowland land now.

"I got the lunch," Margaret laughed. "I told the landlady I was going to meet some friends for a picnic." They set out across the hills, to the southwest, aiming for the first coulee half a mile away that would take them deeper into the Rowland ranch, onto the summer pasture lands, out of sight of the yard and hired hands. For a moment they were visible against the sky if anybody from town should look that way.

They eased their horses down the steep hill into a brush-filled coulee. On the side sheltered from the sun, heaps of snow melted into the wolf willow; on the sunny side, clumps of furry crocuses had pushed through grass as pale and dry as straw.

They let the horses walk, stretching hands to touch across the space between them. At the end of the long coulee, they branched into another running southwest. The sun grew hotter as they rode, nearing its highest point in the sky. Nicu felt too hot in his sheepskin vest, turned fleece inward over his dark workshirt; he took it off and tucked it into his saddlebags, and it seemed that his body was growing lighter in the warm air of spring. Margaret rode with her hat off, the ends of the deep pink ribbons trailing on the wind. They took their time, thinking only of the sun and the hills and the long slow ride.

They came to the foot of a big hill, looked up at chunks of stone that jutted out of the grass, flat and smooth, like huge gravestones, like the stone Chisholm had used to carve his house. They rode single file up a narrow path that curved between the stones. On the hillside they were again visible for miles around, and again they looked in all directions, but saw no one. They looked northeast to the town, at the tiny houses, the steeple of the new brick church.

As they climbed, the hill's curve flattened out and grew to almost fill the sky. Near the top, Nicu felt a thrill of fear, that someone might be waiting for them on the other side, or that maybe there was really nothing there, just a steep drop into nothing. Then they cleared the top and looked down into the valley, the hill smooth and grassy on this side, the valley bottom thick with poplar and willow and tall cottonwoods along the nearly dry creekbed that wound through it. Paradise Valley, the Rowlands called it. Nicu found out about the valley from Paia Manescu, who knew the hired hands on the Rowland place; they told him Mrs. Rowland loved the valley because it reminded her of England.

The grass along the creek was already turning pale green, the rasping voices of crows drifting on the warm air; again Nicu felt the heaviness of winter lifting from his body. Margaret turned and smiled at him, and the sun was in his eyes, and tears were in his eyes. Then she was running her horse down the hill, he following on the smooth-gaited bay mare, his first horse. They headed not for the creek, but for a more sheltered place, a spring in a small clearing where grass grew in thick tufts. They watered their horses in a muddy pool around the spring and turned them loose to graze, seeing in the wet earth the hoofprints of deer. Near the spring was a stone circle, with charred bits of wood from old fires. Maybe Mrs. Rowland came here on picnics.

Nicu watched Margaret unpack her saddlebags, lifting out an old grey blanket, a lunchbox, a quart sealer of lemonade, and setting them down in the grass.

"Let your hair down, Margaret," he said. She raised her arms and unfastened the pins that held the braids around her head; unwound the braids, separating the tight bundles, combing them loose and wavy with her fingers; then she twisted a few strands into a topknot and tied the ribbons around it.

Sun glistened in the soft brown hairs on her arms. She pulled clumsily at the laces of the corset, her face pink, eyes turned down. They faced each other, sitting on the grass with their legs tucked under them. Nicu looked at the strange stiff garment that held Margaret's waist in and pushed her breasts upward. He couldn't help holding his breath, then felt it escape in a sigh as the laces loosened and the corset opened in front. She lifted her arms over her head so he would lift the corset off for her; already the loosened garment fell away from her breasts, and he stared at her smooth skin, creased by the seams of the tight canvas, at the puckering brown skin on her nipples. Carefully he lifted the corset over her head and set it on the grass. He could hear her breathing, quick and shallow like his own.

Nicu cupped her small breasts in his hands, feeling around to the sides and up to the tufts of brown hair under her arms, curling and soft like cornsilk. He unbuttoned his shirt and threw it on the grass. He put his arms around her shoulders and drew her towards him, closing his eyes as her breasts touched his chest. He pulled her closer, till all their weight rested on their knees, and they fell sideways in the thick grass. They stretched out and lay still, Nicu's head resting on her breasts, where he could hear the beat of her heart. He couldn't move now if all Rowland's men came riding up. Margaret held him there, and the feeling in his belly was a warm heavy weight.

A drop of sweat formed under her breast like a growing drop of rain; it trembled for a moment, then trickled down towards her belly. Nicu placed his hand in its path, let it roll onto his finger, then licked the finger, the sweat salty on his tongue.

Margaret was running her hands over his chest, hands brown from sun; he bent to kiss her breasts, the crinkling brown skin of her nipples. The sounds of their breathing, growing faster and faster, seemed to be the only sounds in the world. He loosened the fastenings of her trousers and stroked her belly. He eased the trousers over her hips, she arching her body to help him, trousers and light silk underpants peeling away in a single layer, bending to slip her feet out of boots and stockings.

He wanted to feel the warm air on himself too. He untied and kicked off his boots, then started to ease away pants and underwear, now almost afraid for her to see him. No one but mama and tata had seen him with his clothes off. For a moment he thought she was afraid, but then it seemed to him that she wanted him to hold her, and he peeled away his clothes and lowered his body against hers. She held him tight against her. He could hear his heart pounding, could feel hers; sweetness from her warm skin washed over his body, his mind.

"Margaret?"

She took a deep breath. "Yes, it's all right." She pressed her face into his shoulder. His hand shook as he started to move her legs apart and he couldn't seem to find the place. She took a sharp breath as her hand reached up to him, guiding him; he pushed and felt a yielding, and he was falling, falling into warmth, softness, bright sun dazzling his eyes, trees and sky blurring together. His eyes closed, the silky warmth stroking his mind, his blood rushing. Then he looked at her eyes, watching his face, warm brown eyes, pupils large, bright. His eyes closed again as the aching sweetness filled his belly, and he had to move now, couldn't wait —

They lay together, Margaret stroking her fingers over his back. He could feel the sun. He would get sunburned. It didn't matter. He wanted to sleep and wake up still touching her, still touching that place inside her body. It seemed he would always feel it around him, would always be able to close his eyes and feel the shape in his mind. He couldn't believe how beautiful it was to be inside a woman, and yet it seemed he had always known, always wanted just this.

He felt the coldness of fear in his belly. Was it right to do this with Margaret? She might have a baby. To touch another person in that way a person must be very sure. It changed his whole life, changed Margaret's life too. He had to think about when they could be married, how they could live.

Crack! A spasm of fear and surprise exploded through Nicu's arms and legs, and he jerked away from Margaret as if he'd actually been shot. The sound echoed against the valley walls, then a second shot, and a third, and they grabbed their clothes and blanket and food, and ran for the trees. Expecting bullets to tear open his naked skin, Nicu ran back to grab the reins of the horses, still quietly grazing, and led them into the trees and tethered them to branches. Margaret had her pants on, still open at the front, her fingers fumbling with the laces of her corset, pink ribbons dangling across her face.

Nicu yanked on his trousers, not bothering with underwear, he could stuff that in his saddlebags. Then the shirt. Goddamn the bloody button holes! Margaret sobbed furiously as she finally tied the laces and reached for her blouse. Too late, they could hear a horse crashing carelessly through the brush, snapping twigs as it walked.

Nicu grabbed Margaret's hand and dragged her further into the trees, looking for cover. They crouched behind a chokecherry bush, but Nicu was sure they would be seen through the leafless grey branches. Their hair was flecked with dust and twigs, and a fragment of spider's web clung to the laces of Margaret's corset.

They could see the rider now, a young man on a black horse, carrying a .22 rifle, riding slowly through the clearing. Nicu held his breath, hoping they'd left no signs in the grass. They saw the rider clearly, a heavy-set young man in tan pants that flared out at the hips, a tweed jacket, and polished black boots set in the short stirrups of an English saddle. He was nearly through the clearing. He slipped the rifle into a holster on his saddle.

He reined in and dismounted. What was wrong? He was bending over, picking something up. He put a hand down and ran his fingers over the grass, looked around the clearing, then straight at the bush where they were hiding. His face did not change. Holding in one hand Margaret's silk underpants, he led his horse to a large boulder and remounted. Slowly, casually, he rode towards the trees, towards the bare bush. At the edge of the clearing he stood in his stirrups and hooked the underpants over a branch of a poplar tree, the highest branch he could reach.

Then he rode on into the trees at a slow steady pace, straight towards the chokecherry bush. When he was about fifteen feet away, he gave a wild yell, and spurred his horse, whinnying and rearing, to a gallop. Margaret's scream died away as Nicu dragged her away from the horse's path. The man galloped on past the bush, his laughter ringing in their ears as they ran. They stopped at the creek bed and looked back, saw the man rein in about a hundred yards away, slowly raise his rifle to his shoulder, take deliberate aim and fire; and turning their heads at the sound of the shot, saw the torn underpants still waving on the branch. With another shout of laughter, he rode off, rising and falling in his saddle in the English style of riding, looking to Nicu like some mechanical doll. Nicu and Margaret listened to the big horse galloping through the trees. There was a final shot, echoing through the valley, as if the man had fired straight in the air.

Margaret put on her blouse, now wrinkled and smudged, and tucked it into her trousers. Nicu finished buttoning his shirt, his heart pounding, fingers still clumsy with the tight buttonholes, but making easier work of it now, although his knees wanted to give way.

"It's that stuck-up William Rowland," Margaret said, her voice angry but still shaking. "I could kill him for that. He thinks because his old man owns half the south country—"

"William Rowland, the boss's son?" Nicu asked. "How you know him?"

She spoke scornfully. "He was at our place once with his old man to collect the rent from my dad. You should've seen them. Old man Rowland's the first person I've ever seen stingier than my dad." She looked at their bare feet. Cold from the damp earth was creeping into their bodies, and she started to shiver. They started back to the chokecherry bush where their boots and picnic things were left.

"My dad had this crazy idea—" Margaret stopped suddenly. "You don't think he saw my face?"

"No, we run away from him. He don't know us if he see us again." Nicu hoped this was true. "What crazy idea?"

"Well, he thought if I finished high school in town, and if he got me lots of fancy clothes, I could marry William Rowland."

"Marry that stuffed shirt?" He stared at her in disbelief. "You see the way he ride? You see his saddle?"

Margaret touched his arm. "I don't want to, you know."

She tried to look into his eyes, but he couldn't look at her. He *knew* Margaret didn't want to marry anyone else, but the idea made him feel sick at the stomach.

"And he shoots gun in spring!" Nicu was growing outraged. "What kind of man shoots gun in spring, kills nesting birds with a goddamn .22 rifle?" Margaret was staring at him. "What kind, eh?"

"What kind of rifle?" she asked.

"A .22," he said, and they were both laughing at once, as if he had said the funniest thing. He hugged her, pressing his face into her hair that was tangled together with grass and twigs. Margaret had put her trousers on over her bare skin. Around the crotch of her trousers, a damp spot was forming. He reached into his shirt pocket for the clean white handkerchief mama had given him. Margaret blushed as he handed it to her, but she carefully folded it and, turning her back to him, opened the front of her trousers, and pushed it down between her legs. Then they sat down to put on their boots.

"Me tu, Margaret!" he said, "you going to marry *me*, right?"

Chapter
SIXTEEN

Nicu urged the light-footed mare to a trot. Gheorghe turned his laughing face up to Nicu, his breath coming in excited gasps. They headed out around the garden a second time, down the slope, and the mare broke into a gallop. Nicu held tight around the child's waist. The dog ran beside them. Tata had a hound now, for hunting. Nicu had chosen the bay mare for her smooth gait and her quiet nature. He'd been training her in the evenings after work, and now she responded to the slightest touch on the reins or the pressure of his legs. His work with the mare helped keep him sane during the long days at the yards.

The morning was cool, but a bright sun warmed them, shining in a sky of deep blue with no clouds anywhere to measure distance by. The child's laughter drifted away, high clear notes frozen in the air and in time. Gheorghe turned again and smiled up at him, and Nicu was aware of it all—the sky, the smell of melting snow and wet earth, the child's eyes reflecting sun — and he thought, even when I'm an old man, I'm always going to remember this.

Coming back uphill on the far side of the garden, the horse slowed to a walk; Nicu let her amble to a stop near the trough, slid down, then reached up and lifted Gheorghe in his arms. For a moment he thought Gheorghe was going to cry because the ride was over. But Nicu lifted him down and held him in one arm as he led the bay mare to the trough. She snorted, then drank from the chilly water, still flaked with ice around the edges of the trough. Nicu watched Gheorghe, his whole body concentrated on the mare, and he felt tears in his eyes. Did tata look at me like this when I was small, he wondered?

Still holding Gheorghe in one arm, Nicu led the mare to a stall in the barn and carried hay to her manger. Zaica stamped his feet in the next stall; it wasn't often there was another horse in the barn, especially a mare. In the dim light, Nicu watched barn swallows slice through the air above him, in and out of their nests beneath the rafters, coming so close, but never touching anything. They rode invisible paths, different every time, always controlled and perfect. He loved the muted orange of their bellies. Watching the darting birds, he rubbed his hands against the cold.

Outside in the light, the sun warmed them again. Nicu lifted Gheorghe up to ride on his shoulders; the child made no sound, but Nicu could feel the small hands, rough and red after the winter, on his head, nestling softly in his hair.

Mama and Luba looked up for a moment as they came into the hot kitchen, Nicu ducking low to keep Gheorghe's head from hitting the doorframe. Nicu lifted his brother down, smelling the food the women were cooking for the evening: roasted lamb, roasted chickens, and he was hungry again even though he'd eaten a big breakfast at his boarding house in town. Now they were making cabbage rolls, filling the biggest pot with a growing mound of them, spreading each leaf with meat and rice, rolling them, and tucking the corners in so neatly that the rolls would never fall apart. They worked without speaking, but Nicu could feel their excitement; Luba's cheeks were pink and her eyes shone.

Neither of them stopped to bring him coffee, and he noticed because it was the first time that had ever happened; always a woman, his mother or sister, bringing him food. Nicu got cups and cream and sugar from the cupboard, and the tin that held baking . "Fine Scottish Biscuits," it said, below a picture of low rugged mountains, and close-up, a single horned animal, a shaggy highland bull. They had found the tin in the house when they first moved there. Inside now were doughboys, like doughnuts from the bakery in town, but with no holes, and poppy seed rolls.

Gheorghe sat down with him, and Nicu poured milk for his brother, coffee for himself. Gently he guided Gheorghe's chubby baby hand on the cup.

Already this morning mama had asked him to come home again. He had taken Gheorghe outside to ride the horse to keep from talking about that. He wanted to tell her about his life in town, the brickyard, the place where he stayed — Mrs. Dunkling's boardinghouse. Funny English name, eh? he would say. Listen, he would say, you don't have to heat water for me this time. At Mrs. Dunkling's they have this big tub with running water, hot and cold; a big iron tub shiny with white enamel. Good wells in Coteau, all the water they ever need. I can have a bath twice a week if I want. But mama didn't want to hear about that.

Nicu went to his coat, which hung near the window on a hook made from a deer's foot. He felt around in the pockets and brought out two packages loosely wrapped in paper tied with string. He handed one of the packages to Luba, who had finished making cabbage rolls. She washed her hands and sat down at the table to open it. She felt the package. It was something soft. Something to wear. Luba took her time opening the parcel, picking the knot out of the string with great care.

She shook out the folds and held it up. It was

a blouse of cream cotton muslin, with rows of tucks edged in lace across the top; just like Margaret's, the last one in Lazbee's store. Five dollars, just for one blouse.

"Doamne!" mama cried.

"Ah Nicu," Luba said, "that's very beautiful." She ran her fingers over the close-woven cloth. "Multsam, Nicu. It is too much, too nice."

"I wanted you to have it for tonight. It will look good on you." She blushed again as she folded the blouse and wrapped the paper around it again. "That's good," he said, "don't let Paia see it till tonight."

He handed the other parcel to mama; she stared at it, suddenly embarrassed.

"You don't need to bring me presents."

"I know, I just wanted to." He touched her arm. "It's a long time since I've seen you, maicutsa."

She folded back the paper and drew out a long silk shawl of the colour Eaton's catalogue called ecru, with long corded fringes. The ends were embroidered with wide borders of flowers and birds, tiny birds like the colibri that flashed red and green in the bushes around her tata's house in the old country. Nicu hardly remembered them himself, but mama still talked about them.

"Nicu!" mama cried, "where did you get such a thing?"

"There's a lady in Coteau makes them."

"But the embroidery, the little birds—"

"Just like in the old country, eh?" He laughed, showing his even white teeth.

"Yes, like the colibri—but they don't have them here—"

"You're sure of that, mama?"

"Of course I'm sure. I've been here six years and I've never seen any!"

"Maybe not, mama, but Mrs. Fraser saw them."

"Mrs. Fraser! Who is Mrs. Fraser, I don't know her."

"Now don't be mad, mama, I'm going to explain. I saw a shawl like this in Lazbee's store in Coteau, embroidered with flowers, and I thought, mama would like this." Sofie was getting interested in the story. "So I asked Lazbee where he got such a beautiful shawl, and before he can think, he says, there's a lady in town makes them, Mrs. Fraser."

"I ask him, how much? He turns over a tag, and there's the price: ten dollars."

"Me tu!" Mama's eyes widened in horror, "ten dollars!"

"Wait mama, did I say I paid ten dollars? What I did was, I asked at the livery stable, where does Mrs. Fraser live, and they showed me a little house near to where I'm boarding. So I went there one day after work. And you know what?"

"What? Doamne, what?"

"She asked me to come in; and she brought me tea in a pretty china cup, so thin I was almost afraid to hold it. Mama, such a pretty little lady!" Sofie frowned. "Very small, with tiny bones like the china cup, hair white as snow. This lady must be eighty years old" (mama's face brightened, it was good to speak well of old people), "and she flits around her house like a little bird. In fact that's what made me think of it."

"Think of *what*?"

"Of the colibri. I asked could she make a shawl, and she said she would be glad to, she could use the extra money. That's when I found out what Lazbee pays her. Can you guess?"

"Guess! How could I guess? How do I know how such a man does business?"

"He only pays her three dollars."

"And charges ten? Doamne! that's wicked!"

"It's very cheap of him, all right. So I said I would pay five dollars, if she would make a very special shawl. And I asked if she knew a bird called colibri."

"And did she know it?" mama asked, so interested she forgot to tell him five dollars was also far too much to pay for a present.

"'Tell me what they look like,' she says. So I said, very small, with long pointed beaks, and their wings flutter so fast you can hardly see them.

"And her eyes light up like sparks and she says, 'What you're talking about, lad, is hummingbairrds! Of course I've seen hummingbairds.'" Nicu rolled his r's to show how Mrs. Fraser talked.

"But Nicu, where did she see them?"

"In the garden. She said they like to come to the flowers in her raspberry bushes in summer."

"Maica Domnolui! I didn't know there were such things here. Could it be I wasn't watching, and they were in my raspberry bushes too?"

Sofie had aged since Nicu had been home at Easter. Her black hair, tied in a bun, was streaked with white. He draped the shawl over her shoulders, and her face relaxed as she ran her fingers over the bright patterns, losing the touch of suspicion that had grown there over the years. Again Nicu felt tears strike his eyes. Doamne! Was he going to spend the whole day trying not to cry?

He longed to tell her about himself and Margaret. They were going to be married, and he wanted her to be glad. And yet Margaret was not Romanian; mama would think he should marry a Romanian girl. But he didn't know any Romanian girls except Petrica, and she was only thirteen.

Two shapes passed the window and he heard footsteps in the lean-to. The door opened and tata and Paia came in, their faces lighting with pleasure, as if they hadn't known how happy they would be to see him. Tata came with arms open, hugged him close. Paia grasped his arm. Again, the knot in his throat, and he thought, I might as well face it, I'm going to cry today, and that's it.

Tata was looking him up and down, felt the muscle of his arm. "I think maybe you've grown an inch. Looks like they don't feed you too bad in Coteau."

"Not too bad," Nicu answered, but he wasn't going to tell about the white bread. "Of course the food isn't as good as what mama makes; the English don't have any mamaliga, or cabbage rolls, or placinta."

"Asha!" mama said, "what do they eat then?"

"Oh, a lot of things the same as us—roasted meat, oatmeal porridge, potatoes, carrots, bread—"

"What kind of bread?" mama demanded.

Now how had he let that slip out? "Well, ah, mostly white bread, I guess."

"Mostly *white*! Mostly white, he says. Pentru numele lui dumnezeu! How are you going to live on that stuff?"

"But mama—"

"You will turn weak and thin, like skim milk!"

"But mama—"

"You'll get pale and white, like the English.

Your skin will burn every time you go in the sun."

"But mama, I've seen lots of English people, their skin gets tanned too."

"Listen to me draguts, that's where it's leading."

"Well Sofie, he doesn't look too bad so far," tata said. "Maybe if we feed him good while he's home, and send some mamaliga back with him, he won't do too bad."

"Me tu drac! You're laughing at me. Instead of telling him to listen to his mother. Instead of telling him to stay home with his family where he belongs." She turned her back to him and began stirring a pot on the stove. "Luba," she said, "bring coffee for your tata and Paia." Tata went to the stove and patted her arm as she stirred.

"There, there now, Sofie, I know. But he'll be all right in town. Then one day, when he sees enough of it, he'll come home."

"But all the same—"

"I know, draga, I know. But he'll be all right."

"White bread," mama muttered, "is not fit for dogs." But she stopped stirring and came to the table to drink coffee and eat doughboys with the others.

Paia had lived here since Luba had promised to marry him. Already he had learned all about sheep, and they knew he would never go back to farming. Nicu remembered them coming in the

door, Paia looking more like tata's son than he
did; they where shaped more alike, with slender
tall bodies. He had been glad when Paia came,
because it made it easier for him to go to Coteau
to look for work — mama couldn't say there was
no one to help tata. Now they could do without
him; Paia was a better son for tata than he was.
He felt angry with Paia, sitting at the kitchen
table as if he had always lived there. But he knew
it wasn't Paia's fault. He had wanted to go away;
he could never have married Margaret if he
stayed home, working on her father's place. He
had to get more money.

Nicu went to his coat, felt again in the deep
pockets. "I brought this for you, Paia," he said,
giving him a package.

"Multsam, multsam," Paia said. He opened
the package — a wonderful jackknife, its steel
handle engraved with flowers linked by curving
lines. It had a good blade for whittling. Paia
touched his finger carefully to the sharp edge,
smiling his slow thoughtful smile. Nicu had
watched many times as Paia carved small
animals for Gheorghe to play with. He didn't do
it himself any more, but he liked to watch Paia.

Tata's present was in the porch. He felt their
eyes on his as he went to get it. When tata pulled
away the paper, there was a small block of wood,
reddish wood marked with rippling shapes that
grew from a centre, their jagged lines softened in

the grain. Wood for carving. Tata smiled, his fingers touching the rough block.

"Multsam, fiu mea," he said. "You didn't need to bring us presents."

"I know I didn't." Nicu swallowed. "I just wanted to, it's been so long—"

Tata smiled at him. "You will always be wanted here, my son—always." There was no keeping tears from his eyes, but he held his face calm, nodded at tata.

Nobody moved. There it was again, the creaking of a wagon, jingling of harness. The preacher must be coming early. They expected him at four o'clock, and it was only noon. Sofie went to the window. "Asha!" she cried, and they all ran to see.

Dragging slowly up the hill was a wagon, pulled by a team of sluggish grey horses. A man and woman sat on the high seat, the man lounging carelessly, feet against the sides of the wagon, pointing this way and that. The woman ignored him, watching straight ahead as she drove.

"Asha!" Sofie said again. The man was no preacher. Stefan just shook his head, back and forth, his eyes wide. Luba and Nicu and Paia watched in amazement, but nobody said a word.

The woman sat very straight, holding the reins firmly, as if the horses might bolt if she weren't careful. Her clothes were neat and stylish

— a close-fitting grey coat, matching grey hat on her head. An English woman. A city woman. The man wore a suit, sober black like a preacher, a white shirt, and Dumnezeu, yes! — black and white striped tie. He was holding his legs as straight as he could without falling over, to keep his pants from wrinkling.

The wagon drifted closer and closer to the house, a coloured picture growing bigger and clearer in the frame of the window. Suddenly they remembered their manners, and first Sofie and Stefan, then the others, poured out the kitchen door, bumping into each other in their sudden haste. They stood shyly in a half circle, looking up at the faces of the man and the city woman.

"Hello Stefan!" the man cried, his white teeth flashing in his thin dark face, and jumped down and came around to help the woman down. Trousers flapping around his skinny sparrow legs, he lifted her gently down.

"Hello Musca!" Stefan replied.

"Hello, hello my friends," Musca said; he led the woman forward by the hand. "Stefan, Sofie, like you to meeting my wife," he spoke in English because of the English woman, "my wife Char-*lot* Braith-waite." The woman held her hand out to Sofie and Musca smiled like a man when his cows give pure cream, his ewes give birth to twins, and all his hens are laying.

Sofie and Stefan shook the warm little hand in its soft leather glove. "How do you do?" she asked each of them, but they couldn't think of what to say, it was all too fast. Then Stefan remembered what English people say.

"Hello, hello," he said, "Please meeting you, lady." She smiled at him and went and shook the young people's hands as Musca named them: "Thees Nicu, thees Luba, thees Paia Manescu. And thees little Gheorghe." Gheorghe stared as the English lady kissed his cheek.

"Doamne, come in, come in," Stefan said, and Paia took the horses to the barn. Without quite realizing how they got there, they soon found themselves sitting around the table in the living room, drinking coffee and passing plates of doughboys and placinta. They all tried not to stare at Char-*lot*. It wasn't easy.

She had the most amazing hair, heavy and thick, the colour of wheat stubble late in November when it sticks through the first snow, when it is gold with a tinge of red. Her eyes were the deep blue of sloughs reflecting spring skies. Not a beautiful woman, but oh, so interesting to look at; freckles on her strong slightly crooked nose; nose and cheeks still red from cold.

And her clothes! So neatly made: nicer than from the catalogue. A tailored grey suit and a dark blue silk blouse that matched the colour of her eyes, its ruffled collar framing her face. Not a young face, either — thirty, maybe thirty-five years old.

"But Musca, we don't know you are going be marry," Stefan said with gentle tact.

"Oh," Musca grinned happily, "I not know either, but I'm meeting this lady here," his eyes shone with adoration, "And before I know, we get marry—" and he laughed out loud at this strange thing—"we marry whole month now."

Sofie felt her eyes slide upward, trying not to look below Char-*lot*'s face. Musca's wife was at least five months pregnant or Sofie didn't know anything about it.

Char-*lot* blushed deeply. "You have a very nice house here, Mrs. Dominescu," she said.

This wasn't true at all, but it was something to say while they all tried to adjust their eyes. "Thank you lady," she said. Silence. Sofie tried again. "Very nice clothes you wearing, Mrs. Musca."

"Thank you very much," Char-*lot* said, "I made them myself."

Musca was grinning. "That how I meeting my Char-*lot*—I take my pants to her for fix!" His thin hair was combed across the top of his head to cover the bald spot. His face looked shiny clean, and his suit!—the momaie looked now like a well-dressed city man.

"Asha," Sofie said, trying not to see in her mind a picture of Musca Graba standing without any pants. She was beginning to suspect how Char-*lot* got such a nice round belly. Of course, she could be wrong, maybe Musca had two pairs of pants. Char-*lot* was blushing again.

"You see, I make my living as a seamstress — in Regina. People come to me with work to do."

Sofie nodded. "There is much work to do at sewing to Regina?"

Char-*lot* blushed even more. "Oh, there's enough to make a living. Quite a few ladies like to have their clothes made to measure."

And men too, Sofie wondered? Nobody was speaking again. Char-*lot* was still blushing, Musca still grinning, his eyes running over the very part of Char-*lot* everyone was trying not to notice.

"You got very nice suit there, Musca," Stefan said.

Musca was smiling so hard his head must be aching behind his ears. "I'm telling you, Stefan, things not so bad in this queen town — I got me job, now." His face glowed with pride.

"What kind job?" Sofie asked.

"Janitor, to school — I clean school, fix furnace, stay nice and warm all winter." He laughed with delight at such good fortune. "Now me and Char-*lot* rent little house — good times!" He shook his head back and forth at the mystery of it.

"Pay must be pretty good?" Nicu asked.

A sly look crossed Musca's thin face. "Pretty good, yes, but that's not all. I got some other work brings in little money." He slapped Stefan's arm and laughed out loud—"Some other work, yes"—and he couldn't talk, he was laughing so hard, his voice rising to a high-pitched crooning. Char-*lot* looked embarrassed. "Come on," Musca said, taking Stefan's arm, "I show you."

He walked Stefan outside, their laughter drifting back into the house. They came back and set on the table four glass bottles filled with clear amber liquid.

"My other work," Musca pointed to them. "You see, I come here, and first thing I find, can't get no tsuica here—they never heard about it. So I'm thinking, Musca, God gave you a head and two arms, help yourself. I can get plums only in summer, so now I'm making wheesky." He pointed to the bottles—"Thees for the party. I thought for party, a little wheesky is nice." He was ready to burst with pride. Stefan was looking at the bottles, then at Musca's fine suit, very thoughtfully.

Musca reached into his jacket and pulled out a smaller bottle, setting it on the table between Luba and Paia. "Thees for you, real tsuica, I make last summer."

"Multsam, multsam, Musca," they said together. Luba rose from the table, went to the kitchen, returning with seven glasses. Paia opened the bottle and poured a little tsuica in each.

"My friends," Stefan said, "our congratulation for your marriage—buna sanatate, Musca, buna sanatate, Mrs. Musca."

They raised their glasses to toast Musca and his wife, tasting on their tongues the remembrance of summer and sweet ripe plums.

Chapter
SEVENTEEN

Secrets, secrets. Mama was going to drive her crazy with her secrets. Don't tell this, don't tell that. Don't tell tata. How was she going to remember what to tell, what not?

The secret wedding. Tata was never supposed to know. The priest rode all the way from Kayville where they talk Romanian so strangely. She could hardly understand him. Why had they ever agreed to it? Because mama would never be quiet, never be happy, if they didn't. So there they were, married a whole week before the wedding. Before the Seventh Day Adventist preacher came all the way from Regina. He didn't speak Romanian at all, that one; wouldn't stay for the party, just wanted to get back to town. Pah! mama had said, that's no marriage; no marriage without the priest.

For herself, she didn't care. It seemed to her that the church belonged to the old country, that its teachings didn't apply in Canada. She was a woman, she was kind and strong. It was enough. She was like tata, she didn't need the priest.

Well, they'd had the priest anyway. Tata didn't know. Nicu didn't know. Only Kosma and Nina knew, because they had to go to Kayville to ask the priest to come. Maybe mama was right though. Anyway, they counted from the first marriage. Paia had to sneak into her room that night and each night since, sneaking back again at the first light in the morning. She thought maybe tata heard them one night.

Luba wondered if she might already be pregnant. If she was, the baby might be born before nine months passed. But no one would notice that. Doamne, lots of girls were several months pregnant when they got married. As Baba Sagina always said, the first one can come any time, but after that it takes nine months. What would Baba say when she saw Musca's Char-*lot*?

She checked the pearly white buttons, slowly because her fingers were shaking, to make sure none had come undone. Oh, such a beautiful blouse, how kind of Nicu to think of it. She couldn't wear fine clothes for the wedding with the priest, though. They had to wear work clothes, had to sneak away. They met him at the schoolhouse, had the wedding outside, because the schoolhouse was locked.

The priest had been so hard to understand, stammering with nervousness. Maybe *he* wondered if it counted if you were married outside a schoolhouse; or maybe he expected tata to come with a shotgun and chase him away. But he blessed us. The wedding counted. And even now I might be pregnant. I am a woman now, I knew I could do it. Paia had made her a woman, and she had made him a man. She took a deep breath, and her head felt so light. She should go back downstairs; they were going to dance; Paia was waiting.

Now she knew another secret — Nicu and Margaret were seeing each other in town. She knew as soon as she saw them standing together. Her father thought he'd got her away, sending her to school in Coteau. Thought she wouldn't look at Nicu any more because he only stayed in school such a short time. Chisholm had a big surprise coming some day soon. He probably didn't even know that Nicu was living in Coteau. When he saw tata and Paia, he probably thought it was tata and Nicu; he never looked in their faces anyway.

Mama wouldn't like it. But she'd have to get used to it. What difference did it make if Margaret wasn't Romanian? She would show Margaret how to make mamaliga and placinta herself.

It was getting dark, but Luba could still see her face quite clearly, her shining eyes reflected in the glass of mama's mirror. She raised her hand and touched her hot cheek.

So there was another secret. No one else seemed to realize. Margaret must have told her parents she was going to visit the Langfords. Luba hoped they wouldn't find out the Langfords were here too. She could hear Kosma starting to tune his fiddle. Nicu and Margaret had been standing against the wall, not talking to each other, but any moment they would step forward to dance, and then people would notice them.

The room seemed crammed with people, their warm bodies crowding into the circle made by the lamplight. The table had been moved to the kitchen, to stand beside the kitchen table, loaded with presents and things to eat. The room was getting warmer from people moving and breathing: the Dominescus, the Manescus with Nina's mother, Baba Sagina, who had heard in their letters how nice Saskatchewan was and had come to join them last year; the Langfords, whose daughter Beryl was a few years older than Luba and had always been nice to her at school; Chan, who kept the grocery store in Coteau, stood by the stairs, trying to keep his tall angular body out of the way; Musca stood with Char-*lot*, his arm squeezing her waist; and Margaret, who'd left her house in trousers and changed in a grove of trees into a ruffled dancing dress.

Scree, gree, squeek, went the strings of Kosma's fiddle as he tuned them for the music. Stefan's fingers slid lightly over his flute as songs played themselves in his mind. People stood around them waiting for the music to begin. Even Baba Sagina looked eager. At least sixty she was, but light and strong, never too tired for a little dancing. Or a lot of dancing, Kosma thought, watching her sharp bird-like features, back slim and straight in her tightly-laced corset. Only the Langfords seemed nervous, as if they didn't feel quite at home. English, but very nice people. Their girl Beryl looked good in her green wool dress, a green ribbon in her pretty red hair; too bad about the buck teeth, Kosma was thinking, but a real nice girl.

Wedding presents were spread out on the table. The bottle of tsuica from Musca was already empty, and he had opened a bottle of the whiskey and passed it for people to fill their glasses, although he filled his own twice in between. His wife gave him sharp looks, but he only grinned foolishly. His little black berry eyes gleamed, and already his feet were tapping. By God, he was going to dance! Everyone could see that. And the room was getting warmer, as the fiery drink trickled into their blood. Ah, to dance through that warm air.

Sofie and Stefan had given a small woven rug from the old country, patterned in red and gold, made by Sofie's sister Nadia, the one with the bad leg; white sheets trimmed with Sofie's crocheted lace; and a big iron pot for cooking cabbage rolls. They wouldn't need the pot yet because they were going to keep living with Sofie and Stefan for a while. But at least they'll have it, Sofie thought, when they need it.

Kosma drew his bow over the strings, big hands poised lightly over the fiddle. Kosma and Nina had given a wooden churn and wooden butter molds that Kosma made, one carved with ciocarlie, the lark, and one with the prairie lily; when you pressed your butter in them, it would have the design carved into it. And a cloth, embroidered by Nina with a pattern of green leaves, to make their dresser pretty. Kosma looked at Stefan; they were ready to play. People called for Luba and Paia to come and start dancing. Musca's toes tapped out a beat. He looked at his Char-*lot*'s shiny wheat-stubble hair, her gently rounding belly.

Baba Sagina gave a pillow filled with herbs to help you sleep, camomile tea for when you are nervous or upset, and a tea to drink when a woman is bothered by her monthly troubles. She also gave little bags of fine muslin with sage inside to put in dresser drawers to make clothes smell good. She brought most of these herbs with her from the old country, but some she discovered on Kosma and Nina's place—the sage, and

even the camomile, which she found growing
wild one day, and doamne! no one had even
known to tell her it was there. Me tu! she didn't
know what these young people were coming to,
they didn't seem to know anything.

Stefan and Kosma lifted their instruments,
nodded, and in one smooth movement, began to
play a waltz, a dance everyone would know, to
make their English neighbours feel at home.
Luba was coming slowly down the stairs, Chan
moving aside to let her pass, and Paia went to
take her hand. All at once they were both shy,
but their faces looked so happy they seemed to
shine, made you want to cry. Sofie and Nina
were crying, but Baba Sagina gave them a withering look as if to say, crying, how foolish can you
be! You weren't going to catch *her* crying at her
grandson's wedding, and then, before she knew
it, there was Baba Sagina, trying to hide tears.

Paia and Luba looked down at the floor as if
their eyes were fastened there. He could see her
new shoes, and she admired his fine new boots.
They took deep breaths and looked up into each
other's eyes, feeling the eyes of all the people on
their bodies, their hot cheeks. The room got
warmer and started to spin, and they could feel
the brandy cousin Musca had poured them flowing down into their arms to the tips of their fingers, down into their legs making their feet light.
Luba felt Paia's arm around her, his hand burn-

ing into her shoulder, and she moved forward, carrying the secret knowledge of his body in her belly. For a moment they could not remember how a waltz was danced, then the music pulled them to the centre of the room, and they found they remembered perfectly, their feet counting off the rhythm, one-two-three, one-two-three, round and round the room. Would the dance never end? It ended. They stopped in the middle of the room and everyone applauded, and Musca gave a high-pitched whoop.

The two fathers began to play again at once, another waltz, and Musca stepped over and actually *bowed* to his Char-*lot*, and she let him take her by the hand to waltz. Nicu and Margaret came next, moving slowly around the room, and even inside the circle of warmth that was around her like a soft shawl, Luba noticed how Margaret was shaking, like poplar leaves in the wind, and Nicu too, although he kept his body firm and straight. Luba could feel the other people watching them, Beryl glancing at Margaret in surprise, but she could do no more than look towards them; nothing could pull her out of her own place, where her hands seemed to be growing into Paia's, her husband now twice over, and already something was holding them together, something that filled the air between them. The sounds blurred and buzzed in her head so that sometimes she could hardly hear the music. Then she would shake her head, and the music would come flooding back in, slow and graceful, a waltz.

The music stopped, and again the players began a waltz. Luba couldn't keep track of the time, but it was completely dark outside; it seemed they had been dancing for hours, so close together in the small room, endlessly circling. And now this waltz was ending, and Musca twirled his Char-*lot* around and around. His blood was humming, he wanted to go faster, he wanted to dance. To dance! to jump! to whirl! They would have to go faster.

Chan alone did not dance, and Luba wondered if men and women danced together in China. She would soon find out, because Chan's wife and son were coming. Tata and Paia had lent him the last of the money he needed; money they'd earned this spring, shearing for Chisholm and some of the other ranchers. Chan sat at the bottom of the stairs, with Gheorghe on his knee, watching the dancing. He moved his head slightly in time to the music.

With the fathers playing, there were not enough men to go around, and although Mr. Langford and Musca danced with as many as they could, no one had yet danced with Petrica or Baba Sagina, and it was hard to say which was most impatient, the youngest woman or her old grandma. Baba Sagina hardly controlled her feelings, but Petrica stood against the wall, her long brown hair drawn back from her face and curled in dozens of glossy ringlets, and her dress was shiny gold taffeta with a grain in it like cherry wood or moving water. It was from the catalogue, the material was called moire; its collar of ivory lace made her skin look warm and golden like newly pressed olive oil.

Petrica tried to hold her face calm, but her heart pounded with indignation. It was not pleasant to stand near the door while everyone danced. Really, with her curled hair, she looked as nice as the bride. Nicu was dancing with Margaret Chisholm. It was not right, he should dance first with her — they were almost cousins — then he could dance with the neighbour girls. The dance was ending. Another was beginning. Nicu let go of that girl's hands. He was walking towards her. He was smiling at her, he took her hand. She could hardly breathe, it was happening, they were going to dance. Oh, what relief to be moving around the room, not standing tight and still. His hands were warm against hers. She remembered when they were children sleighriding down the snowy hill, their cheeks bright red from the cold, his arms tight around her waist. Now her face felt hot, and at the back of her neck under the heavy cluster of curls, the skin was damp with fine sweat.

Musca moved across the room, balancing his

full glass of whiskey, and was going to dance with Char-*lot*, whose hand he had just let go a moment before, but Baba Sagina almost jumped out at him, her blue eyes snapping, and he had to give in to her power. She wanted to dance now, and there was nothing he could do. A wisp of Baba's hair escaped from the bun at the back of her head, trailed across her cheek. She was pretty springy for an old lady. Well, maybe not so old; after all, what was sixty years? Now that Musca was nearly forty himself, he could see that sixty years was not as old as he had once thought — as long as you had your health. As he took her hands in his, he felt the wiry strength that was still in her.

Stefan left Kosma to play alone, and led Sofie to the floor. Oh, she thought, he does dance nicely, my Stefan. I hope he doesn't find out about the priest, he'll never forgive me. She looked anxiously at him, and he smiled, thinking she felt sad because her daughter had grown up. "We couldn't ask for a nicer boy for our Luba, eh Sofie?" he asked, and he sounded so kind that she felt ashamed of deceiving him. Oh well, she thought, what does it matter, he will never find out. She was just glad they were properly married. "No," she answered, "we could never have found anyone nicer, and the child of our own dear friends. It is just as we always knew it would be."

The next dance was a polka. Nicu danced with Nina; Paia still danced with Luba; Musca danced with Baba Sagina, because she didn't let go of him. Aha, he was thinking, the polka will tire her and then I can dance with my Char-*lot* again. Stefan danced with Sofie, and Mr. Langford danced with Margaret, everyone bumping together in the small room.

Now Stefan took Luba's hands and danced a waltz with her. They didn't speak, but she could feel his kindness like a centre of warmth in the warm room. She looked into his eyes, and thought how she had never noticed before the depths of eyes seen in lamplight. He smiled at her, and it seemed that he knew everything, the secret wedding, Paia coming to her room, everything. Then she wanted to laugh at herself; he couldn't know, he was just being kind, just himself. And yet...

Soon they must stop to eat; the smell of roasted meat and cabbage rolls keeping hot in the oven was making Musca, for one, feel almost faint. Nicu took his father's place with the flute, and played polkas and Romanian dances, and Stefan danced with Nina, and Musca danced with Sofie, and Paia danced once more with Luba. Mr. Langford danced a polka with Petrica. And then they played a Romanian dance where only the men danced, and now Musca could dance as fast as he wanted, feeling on his body like heat the zamfir blue eyes of Char-*lot*, and his face grew hot and his feet flew like the wings of the colibri.

Chapter
EIGHTEEN

She is walking over the hills, to the poplar bluff in the long coulee. She can't remember why, but she has to reach the trees. It is terribly hot, too hot for walking, and she thinks longingly of the coolness in the trees. She tries to run down the hill, but her belly feels so strange, and then the hills are whirling around her, the ground moving up to meet her.

Lying down feels good, the ground much softer than she'd expected. The hills are all around. They seem to be moving, like a saucer spinning on a table, spinning closer and closer to the sun. Slowly she gets up, the ground flowing beneath her feet. She is walking into the long coulee, walking to the trees. She can see them now, but she never seems to get any closer. She looks up at the sun and begins to laugh, because it has split itself in two, and it's making the hills go round. Her stomach doesn't feel good. A cool feeling prickles across her scalp.

On the ground she sees white stones that pulse in front of her eyes, swelling, then shrinking, as if they are alive. Her head feels hot, pulsing like the rocks, as she walks down the coulee. She thinks of the well at home, the water so cold it makes your throat ache. She needs a drink of water so much she wants to cry. But she has to get to the trees. She has to find someone. And when she reaches the trees she will find a spring and she will drink. So she keeps walking, as the hot sky presses down on her, flowing like syrup over the hills. The wind begins to blow, a low rumbling that grows out of the earth. The white stones are still moving. And again she laughs, because she sees that the stones are really lambs. Her lambs, she has to look after them.

She takes off her red apron and waves it at the sheep. She tries to herd them together, but they run away in front of her. Their feet pound the earth with a drumming sound that is part of the rumbling sound of the earth and the growing wind. The lambs run towards the trees, and she sees that the trees are much closer now.

A man steps from the trees. He is tall and slim, with blazing blue eyes. He raises his arm and waves. Now she knows. She wants to go to him, but the earth shifts beneath her feet. He is running towards her now, calling her name. Suddenly he stops and looks down. The earth shakes and little gashes open around his feet, the grass *tearing, the earth crumbling away. She starts to run. They are so close now. Before they can come together, the ground opens in a wide crack. She sees it in time and stops. She runs away from the crumbling, splitting earth. But the lambs just keep running. Their feet kick up flying clods as they run, some leaping gracefully into the dark hole in the earth, some slipping in, trying to brace their feet as the ground breaks under them. The rumbling grows louder, and she hears the frantic bleating of the lambs all around her. A tiny lamb runs straight towards her and she knows she must save this lamb. She grabs it in her arms and runs, her red apron trailing from her hand. When she gets it safely away from the hole in the earth, she turns to look for the man. But he is already walking away. As she watches, he disappears into the trees.*

She tries to call him, but her voice makes no sound. She hears only the roar of the shaking earth, the cries and hoofbeats of the plunging animals, the gusts of fierce wind. She hugs the lamb to her. She is crying, her tears are cold, she can't see the sun. The sky is grey-blue, filled with clouds that move like a nest of snakes, coiling, uncoiling, chased by the wind. The hills look taller, dark humped shapes gathered around her, like a herd of buffalo. The clouds come closer, rolling down the hills, until she can't see the hills any more. The clouds are torn open by the wind, and a wall of water sweeps across the hills, driven against her body. And she is so cold, only the lamb warm against her breasts, her belly. She must save the lamb.

Jagged lightning stabs into the hill. Thunder rolls back and forth across the valley, until she is sure the hills will burst open. Maica Domnului, she thinks, help me. Again the terrible fire splits the sky, the rain pouring off the sides of the hills and rushing away in streams, almost as if it would wash away the hills. Then something hard and cold strikes her. The sounds change as the rain becomes hail. She is running. The lamb is warm against her, but she is so tired now. All around her, heaps of frozen white pebbles cover the grass. And then Paia is holding her hand and they are running together.

"Luba, wake up." Paia was shaking her shoulder, and she was waking up in her own bed. "Don't be afraid."

"I thought the earth had split open," she said.

"No," he said, "it's only the thunder."

Outside the dry spell was broken and rain was pounding across the hills. Lightning flashed, and she saw Paia clearly. As the thunder crashed, she lay down beside him.

"You're cold," he said, and pulled the covers up around them.

Luba sat on a stone, water rushing over her feet and ankles, shallow brown water almost as warm as her body, the muddy creek bottom soft against her toes. Gheorghe sat beside her, dangling his feet in the creek, watching the rippling water. It was strange, Luba thought, that they had lived here nearly two years and seen only a dry creek bed. The night Luba dreamed of the storm, the creek started to run again. Dry as this land was, the water ran off it in sheets. The morning after the storm, tata had shown her that the land was only wet on top. Scrape away an inch or so, and it was still dry underneath. But at last it had rained hard enough and long enough for the creek to form itself again.

Gheorghe was very quiet these days. During the storm, he had heard thunder for the first time, and now he was afraid to go outside. Luba wanted to help him, but she was changing too. She seemed to be growing larger, and her mind turned more and more inward. She had become aware of a whole new range of life within herself, her body singing. Sometimes she thought she could hear the blood flowing through her veins. She was more aware of blood itself. Her body seemed fluid and graceful, like water in the creek.

Her breasts were growing and changing, tender and sensitive, like two new beings whose feelings must now be considered with her own.

Her belly felt contentment and calm, as though she had penetrated the secrets of life. She no longer had to work so hard at things. She seemed to understand without trying, to have strength and skill for anything she needed to do. She wanted to explain this to Paia, but couldn't find the words. But each night when they went to bed, she felt he understood. When they touched, something flowed between their two bodies. She didn't have to try to find it, just to wait and it was there, sweet and sure; and the more they found it, the more it was there again the next night. Sometimes in the mornings she would look at him sleeping beside her, hearing mama and tata moving in the kitchen, knowing it was time for them to get up. She always woke before Paia, who loved his bed in the morning. She might put out her hand to give him a little shake, and he would open his eyes and look at her. Then she thought there was no need to explain anything.

Another new thing was that she liked to spin. They had always saved spinning for winter. Now she worked mornings in the garden as if in a dream, Gheorghe playing in the willows near by. Then in the afternoon, she liked to come into the cool house and sit at her wheel. Carding fleece she still hated, but spinning was a new delight. Paia had made her a spinning wheel, run by pedalling the treadle of an old sewing machine he bought in Coteau. She would sit for one hour, two, as much as she could save after her other chores, and the carded wool slipped and sifted through her fingers, the spun wool winding round and round the spindle. Her spinning became smooth and perfect, as thin or as thick as she liked. At the end of the afternoon, she wound the wool off the spindle into a thick skein she washed in the basin. Then she took the dried washed wool from the day before and wound it into a big light ball. Ah, the feel of the soft clean yarn. Soon she would take this yarn and begin knitting things for her baby.

Chapter
NINETEEN

Year after year men had dug their shovels into clay, deepening the hole that ate into the hill. The hill was part of the range the Coteau people called Rowland's Ridge. The Cree called them the Thunder Making Hills, because the summer storms came from that direction.

All day the men worked in sight of hills, but always they stayed at the bottom. Except when they stopped to straighten their backs, they saw only the exposed side of the hill, as their shovels bit into clay, clay settling into pores and wrinkles of skin, their clothing dusted with the fine particles. Ten men worked at shovelling clay into iron cars. Different men at different times of the year, because the jobs were rotated to give the men a change.

As the carts filled they were pulled down to the pug mill by two worn-down Shetland ponies that no longer needed the restraint of the leather blinkers that cut off their side vision; they walked with their heads down anyway, sweat turning their matted hair black where the harness pressed against them. Charlie and Susan were the ponies' names, although both were geldings, their names the unkind joke of Lanks the foreman. Charlie was thirteen and Susan was fifteen years old. They had worked in the pit for the whole ten years since the idea of the brickyard had gathered itself together from a mote in the busy brain of old man Rowland.

Ten men shovelled clay under the eye of Lanks, who stood, turning slowly to the four corners of the yard, as if he, not Rowland, owned all this. His duty to see that all the men worked hard was the less difficult of his tasks. He had also to exert his will to hold the yard together, always holding and keeping it in trust for old Arthur Rowland. He had to hold it, or everything would just slide away—men, tools, machines. Lanks held it.

The men shovelled clay, not looking at each other or at Lanks, but they all felt Lanks's eye on them. They were mostly men in their thirties or forties, except for a couple of men not yet twenty. A single thought burned in their minds: "Move along, you bastard—stop watching us." Lanks seemed to feel the hostile intent, for he turned and followed the cart trail down to the pug mill's clashing racket, where knives and rollers ceaselessly cut and pounded clay that came out fine and even, sloppy wet and ready for the molds.

The men felt Lanks move off, as if metal bands relaxed in their minds. His eyes were off them now, but their work rhythm stayed steady, the fraction of slowing hardly visible as one of the older men, Alan, caught the eye of one of the young men.

Nicu had worked at all the jobs now, and the rotation was simply a joke to him. At first the change was a relief, but soon relief gave way, and in his mind he did all the jobs at once. The pounding and grinding of the pug mill was in his head now, even while he was digging clay, and the heat of the kiln that burned clay until it glowed like fire, burning it to a new form, as hard and dead as stone.

He thought of the main street of Coteau, with its neat brick buildings: bank, offices, Lazbee's store, and the two-story school where Margaret was finishing high school. The new Anglican church with its tall steeple, built with bricks donated by the Rowlands. Now some of the merchants wanted to change the town's name to Rowland. He thought about the donated bricks; the Rowlands donated our work, that's what they did, he thought. Nicu spat, and even his mouth tasted of clay.

"Getting pretty dry, eh?" Alan said. "Lunch time soon." Nicu nodded at him.

When he first came to the yard, he'd thought he couldn't stay, the work was so hard and tedious. But Alan said he would: "You think at first you won't be able to take another minute, but you do. And after a while, you get used to it. A man gets used to anything after a while."

And so he stayed. But he never quite got used to it. He wondered if any of them really did. Did Alan still feel as restless as he himself felt? Did his body ache for the six o'clock release, did he long to grab Lanks and beat him until he couldn't keep them working any longer? Did he want to smash the yard and its machines, burying them deep in the earth? Or did men get like Charlie and Susan?

He had to think about Margaret. They were going to get married; they were going to tell her father. Chisholm's face jumped into his mind: flinty little eyes staring into him, suspicious, uncaring. It scared him to think of telling Chisholm, to see that face, hard as stone. How did a man like that make a daughter like Margaret?

Margaret. Being inside her. Dumnezeu! The thought of that softness filled his mind, he was powerless against it. He shouldn't think of Margaret like that now: people might know what they did at Paradise Valley just by looking at his face. Thank God no one would ask him about it, because he couldn't lie. Yes, he would have to say, we did. We did it. Yes.

His back and shoulders felt cramped and his fingers seemed to be growing around the shovel as it bit into the side of the hill. He wanted to be away from this place, and a picture flashed through his mind: the Coteau; hills covered with tough wiry grass; the grove of trees where he saw the horses; the horses, running along the side of the hill, over the crest, disappearing—

Margaret would be eighteen years old in August. Then they would tell her father. That gave him just two months to figure things out.

Nicu realized that Alan was no longer working beside him. He turned and saw the older man walking beside Lanks, who was pointing in the direction of the pug mill. Alan nodded.

Nicu was covered with dust; it made a film of grey on his blue shirt, his brown serge pants. On his face it mixed with sweat on his forehead and upper lip. Lunch time was coming soon. There was a bucket of water where you could wash your face and hands. He pushed his shovel into clay, lifted it high over the cart, swung it forward again. There was a shrill steam whistle, and he stopped in the middle of the swing, the long blast echoing in his ears, flung the shovel away from him into the side of the hill.

"Them sons-a-bitches!" Alan was saying. "Them no-good rotten sons-a-bitches!" He shook his head in disbelief, springing open his lunch pail and pulling out a thick sandwich. "I heard old man Rowland talking to Lanks, and you know what they're goin' to do?" Nicu shook his head, as a tall thin man sat down on the packed earth beside them. Israel. Israel shook his head, opened his lunch pail.

They were sitting on the ground along the brickyard fence in the northeast corner of the yard, the farthest point from the machinery; on the other side of the fence was open grass and a grove of poplar.

"Well, what they figure to do, them sons-a-bitches, is old man Rowland's got it in his head to get this steam shovel." His eyes met Israel's. They had both worked in the yard for nearly ten years.

"Steam shovel?" Nicu asked. "What is steam shovel?"

"Steam shovel's what you get so you can fire men, that's what."

"But how, Alan?"

"Well, I'll tell you." Alan was chewing a roast beef sandwich. He looked around to make sure Lanks was out of earshot. "It's a machine. One part's like a small room, holds the steam engine that runs it, and a man sits in there to work it. At the front there's a big steel scoop with metal teeth on the end, on a long metal arm. The man sits in the room and works the scoop, and every time it picks up a shovel full, it gets a couple yards a clay. Fill up one a our carts in four scoops."

Israel nodded his head, but Nicu looked puzzled. "But how does the man lift the shovel?"

"No, no Nick, you don't understand," Alan said, "he doesn't lift it, the steam engine does all the work."

"How?"

Israel spoke. "The engine is connected to the arm that holds the shovel. The man just presses levers, and the machine moves the arm and the shovel." Israel looked at him so seriously, wanting him to understand, that Nicu thought he could see what it might look like: little wooden box with an engine in it; long arm, metal, with a big shovel on the end; metal teeth. For a moment he saw it, then the pictures slid from his mind.

"But what you mean about firing men?"

"Well," Alan said, "the sons-a-bitches figure if they get this steam shovel they don't need all them guys out there shovelling clay. One a them things'll do the work a ten men. So they figure, that's ten men they don't need."

Nicu felt a coldness in his belly. What if they fired him? How could he marry Margaret then? There was no other work in Coteau, unless he hired on as a hand on the Rowland ranch. That didn't pay enough to keep a wife, and there was no place for a cowboy with a wife to live on the Rowland ranch anyway. They couldn't fire him.

"They couldn't fire me, could they?" he asked. Israel looked at him with sad eyes. Alan turned away, spat on the ground.

"I'm supposed to pass on a message from the boss," he said.

"From Mr. Rowland?" asked Nicu.

"Yeah. He wants some extra hands next Sunday. Seems there's a band of wild horses on his land. The stallion's been stealing his mares."

"Do we have a choice?" Israel asked.

Alan grinned. "Not exactly. He wants three. Randy already volunteered."

"I'm no cowboy," Israel said.

"I saw some wild horses once last fall," Nicu said. "Maybe it's the same ones." He remembered them running away across the hills.

"If the stallion had the Rowland brand on him, it is," Alan said. "You want to come? It's an extra three bucks."

"Not bad pay," Nicu said.

"He figures it'll be worth it," Alan said. "He expects to get all the mares and foals."

"And the stallion?" Israel asked softly.

"Yeah, he wants to get the stallion too," Alan said. "A Rowland can't ever stand to give up something once he's owned it."

"You're talking about horses, of course," Israel said. "Or cattle."

"Yeah, of course I am," Alan said. "But just remember, I went to school with Larry Lanks. He used to be a real decent guy."

Chapter
TWENTY

The men have gathered at the Rowland Ranch, their horses forming a ragged line along the big slough Old Man Rowland calls Lake Eleanor after his wife. Above this slough is the biggest house in the south country, made of stone cut by Chisholm in two years of labour. Below the sloughs are barns, shops, bunkhouses, and granaries. The Rowland yard is built on the highest point in the Thunder Making Hills, and from it you can see Coteau, and even, far away in the east, Chisholm's smaller stone house.

Nicu rides the bay mare. She stops to drink at the slough and he sees her reflection, her dark head with the white blaze on the forehead. He sees himself, sitting squarely in the saddle, gazing down into the sparkling water, blue with colour from the sky. His eyes are drawn down, down to the surface of the water, green algae floating just below the surface, but blurred, out of focus. Wind stirs through his hair, the water ripples, and the picture dissolves beneath his eyes. He looks up and the scene around him comes up to meet his glance, the hills rising towards the sky; the sky so close here, closer than in Coteau.

The horses milling, the men excited, wanting to be off. Young Rowland on that sissy English saddle, boots polished and dark, gleaming in the sun, pulls back too hard on the reins; Nicu sees the metal bite into the horse's soft mouth and the big hunter rears, whinnying, just so Rowland can show off, rising in the stirrups, holding his balance as the horse skitters sideways, digging spurred heels into the glossy flank. Nicu looks at the hard calf muscles of the man pressing against the horse. Bastard, he thinks, his own legs tightening in the saddle.

He smells sage and wolf willow, washed across his skin by a light breeze that ruffles the grass, stirring the air that is hot and dry, that touches him like the dry kiss of the sun. The sun is high overhead. A man is watching Nicu — while Nicu watches young Rowland — a smile touching his mouth, squeezing the corners of his eyes. A man sitting straight and awkward in the saddle, Alan: We're not fooled by that bastard, eh? his eyes say to Nicu.

Old Man Rowland yells an order, and the mounted men gradually form a column, two horses wide. Thinks he's in the goddamn army,

Nicu thinks; that's the real reason they're doing this. Not just to get the goddamn horses, but to have the chance to order a bunch of men around: I can buy you; I can order you. Nicu and Alan join the end of the line, walking their horses south into the heart of the Rowland ranch, as the column heads down into a coulee. The line starts to move faster, and Nicu's horse responds without any visible signal from him, her movement smooth and pleasant against his thighs, his body light and floating on hers, moving in the same rhythm, his balance light and easy. He rides in a saddle, but he doesn't need it, doesn't need to stand in the stirrups for balance. He has all the strength he needs, but he doesn't have to do foolish things to show others.

The sun has moved higher in the sky. The column is still two men wide and Nicu's skin is hot, gritty with the dust the horses' hooves raise in the dry grass, but young Rowland rides up and down the column, close against them, to keep the column tight. He wears a snowy white shirt, has taken off his black riding coat and silly round black hat. He rides so close that the bay mare is distracted and starts to turn her head, but Nicu firmly reins her back. He does not look at young Rowland, although the hatred is working again in his guts; his eyes look straight ahead, his back is straight. This coulee leads down, soon they will be entering Paradise Valley, from the northeast, a half mile north of the way he and Margaret came, through a narrow pass between two hills.

They know the place in the valley where the horses are watering. Lachance, now one of Rowland's best cowboys, rode out earlier to scout them; he came back a little while ago: *the horses are there... it will be very easy... you can get quite close to them before they see you... grazing in a small meadow near the creek... trees all around for cover... the wind is with you... make a line around them so there is just one way for them to run... try to keep your horses quiet... when everyone is ready, just let out a yell and charge them... only one way for them to run, remember... straight down the ravine, and that gets narrower and narrower...*

The men listening to Lachance, his hands showing them, as he spoke, what they would see. Then old man Rowland, his clipped English way of talking: "I want you to catch the mares, at least as many as you can. Try for the stallion, but if you have to, shoot him." (if you have to shoot him. if you have to. shoot him) "But first let Lachance try to get him with the rope."

The rope floats down over the dark head and Lachance quickly loops it around his saddle horn, once, twice, three times, as the stallion pulls it taut, rearing and straining, Lachance still holding the end of the rope in one hand. Nicu watches, hardly knowing what he sees — the screams of the mares, the furious scream of the earth-coloured horse, washing over him, seem to interfere with his sight. The stallion pulls at the rope, Nicu sees the muscles under the rough coat, and all around them the riders are chasing down the mares, roping them one by one, tying the wild mares to trees, and they seem to work their way around him in circles; the grass is being torn and the earth broken by many hooves, dust rising slowly in the air in a drifting brown cloud. Still the stallion rears and pulls on the ropes as Nicu sees flecks of sweat soaking through coarse hair, rope creasing the shaggy neck. "Atta-boy, Lachance, hang on to him," old man Rowland shouts. The stallion is not as big as he remembers, smaller than the thoroughbred old Rowland is riding, as young Rowland watches on his big gelding hunter.

The stallion stops straining and the rope goes slack. He turns and charges at Lachance's horse, little pinto stallion rearing in terror, as the earth-coloured horse raises hooves to tear across its flank; and Lachance so surprised he lets go the rope, arms flailing to keep his balance, the rope slowly unwinding its three loops as Lachance floats downward on the side away from the attacking stallion, his foot still in the stirrup.

And now Nicu sees the stallion running towards himself, his mare quivering under him tries to run away, but he holds her, and the stallion runs towards him, rears in the air not three feet away, rising slowly in a swirl of dust. There is no sound, but Nicu is looking straight at the horse's eyes, as he did on the hillside almost one year before. Then he was a boy; now he is a man. And those eyes seem to look right at him, to know him, again. The stallion turns in the air as gracefully as a dancer, balanced on two legs for an impossibly long time; from the corner of his eye, Nicu sees a blurred white movement, sees the gun raised and steadied, the stallion still on his feet, turning, then the shot so loud it seems to burst in his own head, so long it echoes on and on as the horse turns, then slowly crumples to the ground, blood flung out in a swirling arc from its ruined eye.

The falling horse freezing in front of his sight, he hears the shouts of the men, the screams of Lachance. Two of Rowland's cowboys race after the pinto, and one, Lachance's friend Ouelette, grabs the reins and pulls the terrified horse to a stop. The cowboys leap down and run to Lachance lying on the ground. Again there seems to be no sound until Ouelette starts to slide an arm under Lachance's back: "No, don't touch me — for Christ's sake — don't touch me!" And again at the side of his vision, Nicu's eyes go on working, and he sees the grey colt running down a side ravine, such a narrow place that no one else notices, only Nicu, remembering how the ravine curves, narrowing to nothing as it edges up against two steep hills.

Eleven mares are tied up beneath the trees, along with seven foals. The men have hobbled their front legs and most of them are quiet now, walking back and forth in the area permitted by their tethers, their foals at their sides. They don't even have to tie the foals, because they stay with their mothers. One, a small black mare about eight or nine years old, struggled so hard against her hobbles that she made herself fall over and broke a front leg, so they had to shoot her. They will never get a bridle on her. Nicu thinks of the dead horses, slowly rotting in Paradise Valley, to be picked clean by coyotes and crows. He tries to look away, but can't stop watching the man sent by Rowland to cut off the stallion's long wavy tail, the colour of October grasses.

They make a travois for Lachance from two poles and a horse blanket and hoist him on to it, even though he screams and begs them not to move him. His hips do not look right, something broken there. Old man Rowland reaches into the pocket of his leather vest and pulls out a silver flask, holds it to Lachance's lips. Lachance drinks between gasps, until the flask is empty. Ouelette, who has the gentlest horse, pulls the travois back to the house. The whiskey is maybe stopping some of Lachance's pain, but he no longer holds back his screams, and they hear him for a long time. Soon everything is quiet except for the whinnies of the pacing mares. The dust cloud slowly settles on the men and the horses, on the grass that has been trampled and cut, especially by the iron shoes of the Rowland horses. Nicu's horse is unshod. He nudges his mare, rides her slowly down the narrow ravine. He sees Alan looking after him, knows he will say nothing.

Within twenty yards the thick saskatoon bushes on either side of the narrow gap swallow him up. In one hundred yards he reaches the end of the ravine, choked in tangled bushes. The colt is there, scratched by the bushes, its body quivering as it tries to bury itself deeper in brush. It is the son of the mare that was shot, a dark smokey grey, black mane and tail. Nicu slides off his horse, stands still, letting the colt see him. He takes a step, slow and careful, and it tries to burrow into the brush, but it's not that kind of animal. Nicu holds his hands out, every movement slow as he can make it, the colt watching him. He has time now, it is only a matter of time until he can touch the colt, slip a rope over its head. Then he will rejoin the other men.

Old man Rowland handed the men their money, one at a time, three dollars each. Nicu was last, felt the worn soft bills touch his hand, had to think to make his fingers tighten around them, then slip them into his shirt pocket. His body didn't want to respond, arms and legs felt tired in a way he'd never felt before. I've worked harder than this, he thought: the first week at the yard, the time they'd sheared the sheep for Chisholm; but never before this numbness as if his legs were turned to stone and planting themselves in the earth like the big boulders on the hillsides. His head aching, and every time he closed his eyes, his mind making again the pictures: the dark head turning to meet the bullet; off to one side, Ouelette in his red flannel shirt, mounted on his Appaloosa, watching; and Lachance floating slowly down from his horse, not yet afraid, only surprised, his foot caught in the stirrup; the dark stallion falling, and the faded R inside a now broken circle, the brand Nicu saw so many months ago, before he could read.

Once, when Lachance was courting Luba last winter, he had talked about the days when his people had hunted buffalo. How his own father rode with the Metis freighters from Regina to Wood Mountain. And how his father had taught him to ride horses. Now Lachance might never ride again.

The men were collecting their things and starting to ride off. The sun was just going down.

There was supposed to be a big supper for them up at the Rowland house, but most of the men were just packing up and going home, only the Rowland hands going back for the supper. Nicu was hungry, but he didn't want to eat for a while. He would have to eat soon, but not yet. He mounted the bay mare, forcing his stone-heavy body to rise up into the saddle. Nearly everyone was gone, Alan had gone half an hour ago, and now only the Rowlands, father and son, and a couple of the ranch hands were left. Young Rowland was trying to hang the pale flowing tail over his horse's saddle, and the big horse reared and skittered to keep it from touching him. Rowland handed his son a riding whip.

Nicu turned his horse away from the sight, rode across the meadow and into the trees, through wolf willow and chokecherry, the excited whinnies of Rowland's horse ringing in his ears. When he and his mare were concealed by a grove of poplar, he turned the horse around; everything looked so small, the man trying to master the rearing horse, the old man shouting at him now to give up, the hands staying well back. Nicu reached back for his rifle and slowly raised it, saw the arrogant young face clearly in the twilight, red and angry above the white shirt now streaked with dirt, lined it up perfectly. He lightly touched the trigger, knowing he would never pull it, then was sorry he let it go so far, because he wanted to pull it. His brain spinning like a whirlwind, coming so close, then his fingers easing off, easing off, as he heard a loud command from the old man—"Stop!"—and then the son throwing the reins to the ground, throwing down the whip and the wavy tail, turning his back to them all, leaving the hired hands to quiet the gelding. Slowly Nicu lowered the rifle, his arms shaking, and replaced it in its holster. He got down from his horse and led her further into the trees. This was as good a place as any to wait until they left. Then he would go back and claim his colt and lead it back home to tata to keep for him.

August 1914

Chapter
TWENTY-ONE

The hotel was the only place to drink in town, and like most things in town it was owned by old man Rowland. It was early on a hot Friday evening, sun still blazing outside, but the dim room was cool, its dark panelled walls lit by oil lamps fixed into brackets. Only one other table was occupied, a couple of sheep ranchers having a beer before heading home.

"It's the only way, boys," Alan said, looking into their faces one by one. He spoke calmly, but there was passion in his voice, pushing the words out of him. You believed Alan, he was so solid; tall, raw-boned, no fat on him, but big because of the big bones that stuck out at his wrists and ankles. "It's the only way, otherwise any one of us is out in a minute, and not a goddamn thing we can do."

"Have-a-beer, have-a-beer—erk," a voice croaked with senile geniality as they talked. Their table was already covered with glasses, most of them empty except for the dried foam around the rim.

Israel nodded, but he didn't look too pleased. That one never looks happy these days, Nicu was thinking. He still felt strange with Israel, the first Jew he'd ever known. Israel didn't seem so different from his own family, looked a bit like Musca with dark eyes set around a longish curved nose. He didn't know much about the Jewish religion, but he knew people looked down on Jews in the old country. Israel saw him watching, smiled at him. Maybe he's used to people wondering about him because he's a Jew, Nicu thought, and he smiled back at Israel.

"As you say," Israel was answering Alan, "they can fire us, and there's nothing we can do." Nicu felt the fear in his stomach, even though the beer had relaxed his muscles, like a smooth covering over his arms and legs. "Up till now, though, old man Rowland has never fired anybody without a reason."

"That's true," a man called Randy answered, "he's always treated us fair up till now." Randy was a short stocky man, about thirty years old: he'd worked in the yard almost as long as Alan and Israel.

The parrot sat, claws hooked around the wooden perch, in a brass cage hanging over the bar; an old old parrakeet, older than old man Rowland, they said, belonged to his old man before him, brought over from the old country. It seemed the Rowlands hadn't been quite so fancy in the old country, but now the parrot lived in the bar. In the last few years its brilliant green feathers had faded, its pink collar shading into mottled grey. Ralph the bartender stood and talked to it, weaving conversations around the few things it could say, like "have-a-beer, have-a-beer," and "three's-my-limit-son, three's-my-limit." Ralph was polishing glasses with a cotton towel, arranging them on shelves in front of the big mirror; Ralph kept things very clean.

"Yeah," Alan said, "up till now. But even so, you do the job exactly the way he says, and you get paid exactly what he says."

"Ain't that how it works when you got a job?" Randy asked.

"That's how it works here," Alan said. "It don't have to be like that."

"What you mean, Alan?" Nicu asked.

"When you got a union, you don't just take what the boss offers you. You got a chance to bargain."

"What is bargain?"

"The boss says what he'll give, you say what you think you should get — then you bargain."

"But old man Rowland's always been fairly decent," Randy said. "It ain't him that bothers me, it's that goddamn Lanks, always breathing down your neck. Ever since he came—"

Israel's face had that look of knowing what was happening, but almost hating to say. "You think Rowland does not know what his foreman does?" he asked quietly.

"Well—"

"He knows. He is paying him to be like that. He is paying Larry Lanks to watch over us, to watch over his property. He is paying so he doesn't have to do those things himself."

"You see, Randy," Alan said, "maybe it wasn't too bad up till now. But old man Rowland's been cooking up something new. And it ain't Lanks's idea neither. See, he's been reading up about brickyards in other places—Ontario, the States— and he finds out they got something he ain't got. Does the work a ten men. I heard them talkin' about it the other day."

"Jesus!" Randy said. "Rowland wouldn't fire me, though, not after all this time."

There was a loud croaking and squawking and swishing of wings as Ralph opened the brass cage and threw in a handful of birdseed; like chickens squawking after their food; then the voice of the bird, almost human, "thanks-a-lot-Ralph, erk-thanks-a-lot." It cracked the seeds with its long curved beak. The fat man watched the bird eat, unconsciously rubbing his hands along his apron and nodding at it.

"Maybe not," Alan agreed. "He'd fire the youngest guys first, ones who've put in the least time in the yard." He didn't look at Nicu, who felt his stomach tightening again. The beer was making him feel sick; if he had any more he'd have to run outside and throw up. "Have-a-beer —erk, have-a-beer," came the singsong voice.

"Well, that's fair, isn't it? Let the ones go who've been there the shortest time." Randy wouldn't look at Nicu either. "It's fair, isn't it?"

"I suppose it is," Alan said slowly, "supposin' somebody has to go."

"But it's not our decision, is it? I mean, Rowland owns the goddamn company. He can do what he wants with it, can't he?"

"Not if we have a union to give us some say." Alan looked to Israel for support.

"We could negotiate about that too if we had a union," Israel said.

"But why should I worry about getting a union?" Randy asked. "I'm pretty sure they're not going to fire me. So a few guys have to go, what's the problem? These young kids never stay long anyway." Nicu's fists clenched and unclenched. What was this man saying? That it didn't matter about young men like him?

"Randy has a wife and three children," Israel said. Nicu looked at him, trying to understand. What did that matter? Israel also had a wife and children.

"Thing is, Randy, maybe they won't get to you this time, but this won't be the end of it.

They'll think of something else." Alan looked straight into Randy's eyes.

"Oh yeah, sure." He looked away.

"And maybe if you stand for it this time, they'll push a little harder next, make you wait a few more years before you get a raise. 'Don't worry about Stokes,' they'll say, 'he won't make trouble'. No, maybe it won't be you this time."

"But goddamn it, he's got a right to run the place how he wants. If it was mine —"

"It ain't ever gonna be," Alan said. "And just wait till he thinks of a new way to raise his *profits*. Think he'll care if Randy Stokes has been working for him for five, ten, fifteen years?"

"But he's in business to make profit. How else would guys like us get jobs?" Randy asked. Israel and Nicu sat back, watching the others argue.

"I'll tell you one thing, Randy, we could run that goddamn yard without either a them sons-a-bitches. And Rowland's got back every penny he ever put into the yard, and a lot more besides."

"I still say he's got a right —"

"To do what he likes with us? You, me, Nick? Or maybe you were thinking of being foreman some day?"

"No, dammit! At least, if I ever was, I wouldn't do it like Lanks does."

Israel shook his head. "That is what you think now, Randy. That is not how it would be." Randy made no answer. "And you say it is all right if he fires Nick and the other young men?" Israel spoke without anger, but his voice had more effect now than Alan's.

"I'm sorry, I didn't mean that." Randy looked down at the table.

Ralph looked over at them sitting with serious faces over empty glasses. The parrakeet pecked away at the seeds, its cage swaying with the movement, the perch clicking softly as it moved back and forth. "You fellas want anything more, or you just gonna sit there jawin' all night?"

They turned to look at him and saw that other tables were filling with farmers and townspeople. They realized their table was too near the bar; people were looking at them. "No thanks, Ralph," Alan said, "looks like we'll be on our way soon." The bartender nodded. Alan waited until the people at the surrounding tables were absorbed in their own conversations, then spoke in a much lower voice.

"Listen," he said, "if you boys agree, I thought I'd take the train into Moose Jaw next Sunday. I read in the newspaper where they got this guy there that organizes unions. Thought I'd ask him to come down and talk to us." He waited.

"O.K." Israel said, "if he comes here, I will listen."

"Me too," Nicu said. They all waited, not looking directly at Randy.

"Oh, all right, I guess so. Now do you mind if

we get the hell out of here before—"

"You boys mind if I join you?" a voice asked, and they jerked around. Lazbee, the general store owner; Lazbee, running for mayor and always ready to do a favour for old man Rowland. He was pulling up a chair.

"Actually, we—" Alan began. Lazbee sat down, nodded for Ralph to bring him a drink.

"I was just reading a copy of the Moose Jaw paper," Lazbee went on. The other three stared at him. "Says here there might be a war in Europe."

"There might?" Randy asked, fidgeting uncomfortably.

"Yes, it seems the Serbians murdered the Austrian archduke. You never know what these foreigners are going to do." He stared at Nicu.

"What's that got to do with us?" Alan wanted to know.

"Well, nothing, I suppose," Lazbee said blandly, "but of course, you know, the war may spread—"

"Let us hope not, Mr. Lazbee," Israel said quietly.

"Indeed, let us hope not. But Canada may have to come in." Ralph set up a whiskey for Lazbee. "You boys like anything?" Lazbee asked.

"Actually, Mr. Lazbee," Alan said, "we were just on our way when you came in. I'm afraid we have to move along."

"Oh, that's too bad," Lazbee said.

"Yeah, it's too bad," Alan said, "but some other time we'd really like to share a glass with you." Alan, Israel, Nicu, and Randy reached for their caps, placed them on their heads, pushed back their chairs.

"Another time it is, then," Lazbee said, nodding.

"That's right, another time. Well, so long, then," Alan said, the others nodding. They felt as sober as if they'd never touched the beer.

"Come-again-boys — erk, come-again," came the singsong voice, thin and emotionless, dissolving in a flurry of cackling mechanical laughter.

Chapter
TWENTY-TWO

The pick swings up, arcs down, and the ice is so hard the blow recoils through the man's arms and back. He smashes, again, for the point where it will crack, shiver into smaller blocks. He wants badly to crack it, to finish this job, with so many men and boys looking on. The ice is seamed and bubbled from slow freezing, and faintly amber, covered in dirt and bits of straw from the icehouse.

Another man swings a wooden bucket, sluicing water over the battered blocks, washing away the dirt, and children's arms reach out to catch the flying drops. The pick smashes down, not splitting the block, but at the top splintering the surface to jagged lumps and shards the children grab between blows. Don't eat that ice, a voice says, don't you know it's from the slough? The ice is not for eating but to cool ice cream being made in hand-cranked freezers. Nicu, walking slowly around the fair with little

Gheorghe holding tightly to his hand, knows how the ice is kept under bales of straw in the icehouse, but still wonders how it can last so far into the summer without melting.

He turns, and knows at once she is looking at him. He feels her eyes before he sees her. She is standing at a counter with her parents. Her father is trying to win a prize throwing darts. Her eyes laugh at her father, a secret she shares with Nicu. Even when he isn't looking right at her, he sees the deep rose colour of her dress, like the wild roses in the ravine. He sees it outlined against the sun, against mama's bright shawl.

A small boy sits on a chair over a vat of water. Men throw balls at a target. If they hit the centre of the target, the boy falls into the water. Nicu knows Margaret is watching him now. He knows he can hit the centre easily. He pays money for three balls. The first ball thuds against the edge of the target, but the second is right on the mark and the boy disappears with a splash into the water. In a second the small wet head appears again, lips bright red, but the boy is shivering. Nicu suddenly feels sorry, turns to where she is watching. He smiles and shakes his head. But it's at least ninety degrees today; in fact, the vat looks pretty good.

Everywhere he goes, her eyes are there, and it seems there must be something that connects them. If someone crosses the path between their eyes, won't they be stopped? Won't they feel the energy that passes between them? Or maybe it's heat — won't they be burned? For now, this waiting and watching is all right, but he wants to talk to her, to touch her. They are going to live together soon, he knows that now. Soon everyone must see it. This is not just something they want, but something that must be. Their bodies already fit, their eyes already join together.

He notices Gheorghe looking up at him, mouth bulged out at the side with some ice he has picked up from the ground. "Me tu!" Nicu cries, "don't suck that, it's cacat!" And he reaches a finger into Gheorghe's mouth and pops the ice out onto the ground. He has to laugh at the way Gheorghe's face falls, as though he has lost a great treasure. Then Gheorghe is laughing too, his eyes looking up into Nicu's.

Except for one time when they took lambs to the fair in Regina, Nicu has never seen so many people. People from Coteau and other towns nearby; people from the farms. And the men from the yard are here — old man Rowland has given them the day off, without pay of course. Randy is here, with his three children and his wife. Watching her slight figure, Nicu sees there is another child on the way. The loose brown jacket doesn't quite hide the roundness, but must be making her so hot. Her faded brown hair blows in the hot dusty wind of the fairground.

The smell of dust is everywhere, and the smell of sweat. It seems to Nicu that his own smell is no longer separate, but mixed in with the smell of the other men.

Nicu gives money to a man offering pony rides. He lifts Gheorghe onto the Shetland pony, and the man leads it around a circle three times. When the ride is over, Gheorghe just looks at him, his body tightening. Nicu hands over another five cents, and a small sigh escapes the child as the man leads him round again. Gheorghe is too young to know that the ponies have no spirit left. They are the ponies from the brickyard, Charlie and Susan, lent by old man Rowland, since there was no work for them in the yard. Christ, thinks Nicu, why couldn't he let them rest? It seems to Nicu that the pony takes a long time to walk around the circle; to Gheorghe it must seem too fast. He tries to see the pony's eye as it goes by, an eye shaded by long blonde eyelashes. The pony looks straight ahead although today its black leather blinkers have been left off.

Two more times around, and the ride will be over. Nicu looks at the patient old ponies and feels sad. Then he remembers the grey colt, safe at home with tata. He looks after the colt whenever he goes home for a visit. Some day it will be a beautiful stallion.

He sees the rose-pink dress again over by the

gambling wheel. She is watching her brothers betting on the numbers. Then the wheel turns, clickclickclick, whirling, then slow, ck-ck-ck, stops and then she claps her hands together. They have won, and laughing, take their money and walk away from the fairground, in the direction of the hotel. He feels jealous, she should clap for him. He wills her to turn and look at him. Gheorghe is coming around on his last circle; she turns and her arm comes up, but her father is walking towards her, and she doesn't wave.

He wants to talk to her, isn't quite sure why he couldn't just go over and talk to her, but something still holds them back. Tomorrow she will be eighteen years old. They have agreed that tonight at the dance, he will come and ask her. They will dance together in front of everyone. Tomorrow they will ask her about him, and she will tell them. We are going to be married. I am eighteen years old now and we are going to be married.

He turns to lift Gheorghe down, feels the muscles in his brother's arms, and thinks of a small bird; but Gheorghe is warm, and he gives the boy a little hug as he lets him down.

They walk over to the gambling wheel, Margaret and her father walking the other way, back to where her mother is looking at aprons and tablecloths and other hand-made things on a table. Maybe they will see mama's tablecloth, embroidered in red and yellow on creamy linen; it has a blue ribbon on it; it means mama won a prize, two dollars. Gheorghe's hand is in his; they come to the wheel. It has a scratched wooden counter in front where men lean forward to place their bets. The wheel is a huge pie cut into tiny pieces by metal rods, the sections coloured alternately green and black, each with a number along the rim of the wheel. He bets twenty-five cents on the number eighteen, a silly bet, and for a moment his stomach tightens; he has wasted the money. Other men, hard brown arms resting on the counter are betting on other numbers. The man running the wheel turns it, a clicking blurr of dark green, then slowing, slowing. He looks for his number, there it is! There is a flexible peg that slows the wheel, it will stop on one of the numbers. Eighteen! The man gives him two dollars. Lucky eighteen!

He turns to look for Gheorghe; he isn't there. Nicu spots him over by the blocks of ice. He runs after him. Gheorghe sees him and quickly bends and grabs a chunk of ice and pops it in his mouth. Then before Nicu can grab him, he spits it out on the ground and then bursts out laughing. Nicu laughs too, although he knows he should scold Gheorghe about the ice. Oh, what the hell, he thinks, Gheorghe isn't going to die just because he had a piece of slough ice in his mouth. And he's just a baby, so he can't understand that it's dirty.

He takes Gheorghe's hand, and they go to look for mama and tata. In the poplar trees along the fence, people sit on the grass, eating lunches. At the edge of the trees he sees his family sitting on a blanket. In a moment he and Gheorghe are sitting with them. He wants to take off his boots and feel the cool dusty earth against his feet. He decides that yes, he can do that, and soon his feet are bare. He feels the cool ground, and the air moving over them, and he thinks how good it is not to be at work.

Mama and Luba are dishing food from a big straw basket onto saucers. Slices of cold lamb, buttered mamaliga, a grainy coldness against his tongue. He is so hungry that he finishes before anyone else. Mama hands him clatita — thin pancakes spread with jelly and rolled up — and they seem better than he can ever remember. Mama feeds Gheorghe, but he still gets jelly all over his chin. It's good to watch him eat things — all his feelings show on his face. Does he himself ever look like that, Nicu wonders, with everything passing through his mind pictured on his face? He hopes not. Through a fringe of branches and leaves he looks around for Margaret, sees the rosy dress, the glint of sun on dark hair. She is looking at cakes and cookies on the bake sale table. Mama hands him clatita again, and he has to eat carefully to keep the jelly from falling out the ends. Coolness seeps up from the earth into his body. A bit of jelly falls on his foot. Gheorghe flicks it off with his finger and eats it, giggling.

He looks at Luba, in her wedding blouse. Sleeping at home in his old room, he heard her get up early in the morning to wash. Even now in the dust and heat she smells of soap and faintly of sweat. She eats her clatita delicately, careful not to spill jelly on the ruffled muslin. Luba is also alone at the fair. Paia has stayed home to look after the animals, but he will come to the dance later. Luba is looking at him now. She knows, he thinks, about Margaret and me. But it's all right. She's known for a long time, and has never been against them.

Near by he hears the chink of iron on iron, the chunk of iron on sand, as men play at pitching horseshoes. Tata watches with eyes narrowed against the sun; Nicu feels how he wants to go play this game, sees in tata's eyes the belief that he will be good, can throw anything cleanly and accurately. Tata thinking how he will get his own horseshoes, make his own pit at home. Then next year, he will come to the fair. He will play too. And everybody will ask, who is this man who is so good at horseshoes? We've never seen him play before. Strange, he never thought you could tell another person's thoughts.

At the end of every day, before he goes to sleep, he closes his eyes, and always he can see something from what has passed during the day.

At work it is most often the clay in the hillside, the shovel biting into clay. At home it is wiry strands of grass and the rounding shapes of hills. He closes them now, to see if this trick works in the day; sees: ice, cracked and dirty, shattering into long splinters, scraped to slush; water sluicing, rinsing ice; ponies going round and round; a memory of the smoke-grey colt, running; and melting into each picture, a dress coloured deep rose, and the back of her dark and beautiful head.

Chapter
TWENTY-THREE

The saloon of the Rowland Hotel was transformed. Most of the tables, along with the faded green parrot, had been moved to the billiard section, the rest pushed against the wall. The bottles were gone from the shelves behind the bar, the polished mirror reflecting vases of purple and gold irises around a huge glass punch bowl, its carved edges flashing tiny rainbows of light, the bowl filled near to the top with lemonade. In the centre of each vase of irises were little British flags of stiff material, attached to round wooden sticks. Women moved around the room, placing jars of sweet peas on the tables. A tall red-haired girl, Beryl, was adding chunks of ice to the lemonade, her dress coloured bright yellow like the thin slices of lemon floating in the bowl.

Near the bar, a wooden platform had been built, trimmed around the sides with cloth striped in red, white, and blue. A pair of crossed flags hung on the wall over the platform; paper streamers coloured like the striped cloth were fastened in twisting shapes along the walls and ceiling. On the platform, a three-piece band from Moose Jaw was setting up: a piano player, a drummer, and Jimmy Menzies, the best fiddle player in the south country, listening for an A from the off-key school piano. The room cool, polished, smelling of wax and flowers, the lamps along the wall glowing warm.

People were moving in from the fairground, some with children and babies, women in their best dresses bringing their gifts of food to the long table: light sweet cakes, pies with crisp brown crusts, their thick juices bursting from patterns of leaves and stems cut in pastry, over strips of pastry woven like baskets, edges singly or double crimped, chunky potato salads thick with cream; jellies, breads, pickles, bottles of fruit cordials reflecting in winey dark colours the light from the lamps. Men in shirt sleeves, still sweaty and dusty from the fair, and men in suits who lived in town and had gone home to change. Like Dr. Bentley, looking dignified with his stiffly brushed hair, his well pressed suit. And men who'd spent the afternoon in the saloon before it closed at seven o'clock — the town council had decreed that no liquor would be served at the community dance. The afternoon drinkers could be recognized by their flushed cheeks and too careful walks, and by the soft bulges in their jacket pockets.

Nicu stood with his family in a corner of the room watching the people arrive. There was Randy Stokes and his wife; Israel and his wife Rebecca, thin and delicate like him, olive skin so fine it seemed translucent, seemed to glow against her dark crimson dress. And Alan, in a dark blue suit, came in and nodded to him, then stood alone near the door; he had no wife, although people in town said he had a child in Moose Jaw, a boy. Slowly the room filled with people, their smells and sounds; the colours of women's hair, glowing red, gold, brown, and the white or greying hair of older women; their dresses with ruffles and laces and crisp white pipings, their perfumes, their sweat; men's sweat; the smell of sweet peas, and from outside, the smell of meat roasting. Old man Rowland had donated a steer, and it had been baking in a pit of hot coals for the supper later in the evening. Smells washed over him, colours of dresses and flowers, but where were her eyes, where was the deep rose of her dress? What if her parents had decided not to stay for the dance?

There was a hush, people flowing away from the door to make space for a family entering the room; the Rowlands, walking slowly forward, as if they had all the time in the world; old man Rowland nodding, smiling to everyone, even Nicu. And he wondered, does that bastard even know who I am, that I'm one of his men?

Rowland walking beside his wife, his son William on the other side, each of them keeping free a little space on either side of her, room for her wide skirts. So we can get a good look at her, Nicu thought. He had never seen such a dress: pale purple silk, wide sleeves flowing out around her slim arms, gathered to tight cuffs; long full skirt swelling out to flounces at the bottom, one on top of another; cuffs, low neck, waist, flounces, all were bound in narrow strips of deep purple satin. Hair flowing up away from her head, waved and curled, so high she seemed taller than old man Rowland; bunches of violets tucked into her hair, pinned to the front of her dress. She must be forty-five years old, but she wore the dress of a young woman; she didn't nod and smile, just bent her head a little, only the corners of her mouth smiling, eyes cold and calm, circling the room. Rowland and his son, in their white shirts and white linen suits, looked as cool and perfect as she did; as if nothing must touch that perfect cloth; they seemed the coolest and whitest things in the room. They sat down at one of the tables near the band platform, and the girl in the bright yellow dress turned, went to the bar, brought one of the vases of irises to their table, taking away the sweet peas. No Beryl, don't do that, Nicu wanted to tell her. Angrily, he looked away from them.

He looked at his own family. Mama wore the

shawl with the birds over her plain black dress; Luba was still waiting for Paia, and as she turned to look at the door, he walked into the room. Nicu watched, feeling the attraction that flowed between them like honey, proud of his sister, her dark skin and eyes set off by the pale muslin of her wedding blouse. Her flushed face, and her body, were rounder and plumper than in spring, and Nicu suddenly knew she must be pregnant; he saw tata watching them too, and was almost certain he was thinking the same thing.

The piano player ran his fingers up the keyboard, and Jimmy Menzies tucked his fiddle under his round chin, drew the bow over the strings in a thoughtful way; they nodded at each other; the drummer played a soft roll, and the three men seemed to draw together on the stage. They looked around for a signal from someone to begin. Old man Rowland was nodding to a man in a light summer suit of fine material, who was just entering the room; Lazbee, the newly-elected mayor, stopped and returned a respectful bow that showed the bald top of his head to the whole room. His hair and long side whiskers were cut and brushed to smooth mounds; his clothes, the best of his own store, covered with concealing softness his rounding paunch. He hurried to the platform, spoke low to the band, turned to the waiting people.

"Ladies and Gentlemen," he said as the room

grew quiet (where was Margaret?), "we are ready to begin the dancing, but first, I would like to ask Mr. Arthur Rowland, who has done so much to make this occasion possible, to come forward and say a few words." He looked to the Rowlands' table, clapping softly.

People applauded, and a look of surprised pleasure spread over Rowland's face, as though he had never considered he might be asked to speak. In a few precise steps he walked to the platform, standing solid and tall in front of them, arms held high to receive, then quiet, the applause. Nicu stared at the perfect sparkling white of the cloth on those arms. He heard movements at the door, turned, and it was the Chisholms. Margaret smiled at him.

"Thank you, Mr. Mayor," Rowland was saying, "I am honoured to be asked to speak to you here tonight." He stopped, as if thinking what to say.

"My friends," his voice came slow and deep, "it is indeed an historic occasion which we have gathered to celebrate tonight. For not only does our party mark the anniversary of the incorporation of our town some eighteen years ago, but it may also fittingly commemorate the happy day, almost nine years ago, when our fair Saskatchewan entered the vast and fruitful Canadian Confederation." A few men cheered. "By that strange coincidence of numbers which sometimes occurs, our town is almost exactly twice as old today as is our province." Polite applause, and again the dazzling white arms were lifted.

"I am very happy on this occasion to have the privilege of making this room — which I must confess has seen other uses — " he gave a knowing laugh, "available to you, my fellow citizens, on this happy and historic jubilee." Scattered applause, but he went right on: "I only hope it will be my privilege to do so again and again in future, as long as either I or the Rowland Hotel may endure here, and I am certain my son will want to keep this fine tradition after I am gone..." Face pink and shiny with pleasure, Rowland walked back to his seat, his last words drowned by applause, the son, too, rising to applaud the father's words. Eighteen years, Nicu was thinking; tomorrow Margaret will be eighteen years old.

"Thank you, Mr. Rowland," Lazbee was speaking again. "It only remains for me to officially welcome everyone to our party, and," his voice rose with excitement, "to launch our celebration in proper style, I invite you all to come forward and receive a piece of our eighteenth birthday cake." Three women were pushing forward a carved walnut tea trolley holding a layered cake six inches high, two feet long, covered in icing and topped with a replica in sugar and coloured almond paste of the town's main street. The brick buildings were done in chocolate, the bricks picked out in white icing, and eighteen tall candles burned along the model street, like the street lamps in a big city. "Here it is, Ladies and Gentlemen," Lazbee was saying, "and I know you'll all want to thank the Church Ladies for this gorgeous construction, which I'm told, took two weeks to bake and decorate." The now warm room echoed with applause, as the Church Ladies stepped forward, flushed with triumph, making awkward half-bows to the corners of the room. Adults and children lined up for the pieces of cake, which the Church Ladies were now cutting and handing to young girl helpers who put them on plates and added scoops of home-made ice cream. The first servings were carried to the Rowlands' table, and as each burning candle was removed from the cake, it was fitted by one of the Ladies into a candle holder and placed on the bar, each candle reflecting a twin light in the bar mirror. The mayor nodded to the band, and they began to play a waltz.

People looked to the Rowlands; old man Rowland rose and bowed to his wife, who placed a slender hand on his arm. As they walked to the middle of the floor and glided smoothly into dance, William Rowland, too, crossed the floor and offered his hand to the woman he had been watching, Margaret Chisholm. For a moment she just looked at his hand, then as her parents both nodded, moved forward to accept it.

Nicu stared. He hadn't had time to move, and now he felt he was suffocating. William Rowland's hand rested on Margaret's waist, guiding her around the room, one-two-three, one-two-three, he could feel the beat in his head, could feel his own hand touching her. Why had he been so slow? As they turned, she caught his eye, her shoulders and eyebrows rising in the tiniest shrug, to show him she had only accepted out of politeness.

He tried not to watch, then gave in and watched. He longed to fling the hand away from Margaret's waist; the hand of a man who shot breeding animals in spring, who beat horses to show his power over them. Why, oh why, hadn't he killed William Rowland when he had the chance? He looked at her parents, their faces smiling their satisfaction. Paia and Luba waltzed by, not dancing close, but he could feel how they were held together and was jealous, then ashamed of his jealousy. He looked at Margaret; her face was flushed.

He must be ready when the music stopped. He would go and ask her, even though Chisholm would be watching, as soon as Rowland let go her hand. The music was stopping; they were at the far side of the room by the bar. He did not let go her hand, was speaking to her, leaning towards her; the music began again, and without even asking, Rowland led her again to the floor. Nicu watched, his cheeks burning. They were talking.

Again they were near the bar when the music stopped. William Rowland picked up a glass of lemonade, handed it to Margaret. She lifted it to her lips, and Nicu was walking towards them. Someone moved in front of him, not seeing him.

"Say there, young Rowland," Lazbee was saying with a smirk, as if he and Rowland shared some secret, "this isn't fair—you can't keep the prettiest girl in the room to yourself all night. Miss Chisholm?" He bowed, with a self-satisfied smile, but before Margaret could answer him, Nicu stepped forward, just in front of Lazbee.

"Margaret, you like to dance?"

Margaret looked from one to the other; she was blushing, didn't know what to say. He was sorry, but she had to come with him. He looked straight at her, feeling the eyes of Lazbee and Rowland on him, refusing to look at them. That pig of a Lazbee with his fat belly wanted Margaret. The bastard.

"It's young Dominescu, isn't it?" Lazbee was saying. "Your family live out on the Chisholm place, I believe." His tone was polite, uninterested.

Nicu gave him a slight nod, turned again to Margaret.

"And an employee of the brick yard, if I'm not mistaken?" William Rowland said, with what seemed a knowing smile. Nicu glared at him. The music was starting.

"Margaret," he said again, "you like to dance?" And he took her arm and led her to the floor. Margaret was blushing deeply, her body stiff with embarrassment. People were watching them. They danced awkwardly, not looking at each other. Slowly more couples came out on the floor; Nicu wouldn't look to see if her parents were watching. He gave all his energy to the music, to moving around the floor in time.

Little by little their bodies relaxed, and she was able to look at him. He was aware of his hand around hers, the warm sunny smell of her hair, her breasts under the rose coloured dress. And he felt all his anger float away; holding her, not too close, but gently, firmly, the space between them like a part of their joined bodies. The thing they were together moving so lightly, so gracefully, like bright coupling dragonflies, circling the room, so perfect, the happiness of it might burst his chest; so perfect that for a moment he closed his eyes and thought of nothing else.

The music slowing so soon and he wasn't going to let her go, danced her towards a corner, still holding her hand, not talking, waiting for a long moment. Then the music beginning again, releasing them to movement, and this time he heard the high sweet notes of the violin. And thought, they must be watching, her parents, Lazbee, young Rowland. He didn't care, he was so proud; Margaret was going to be his wife, and now everyone would see they belonged together. And this time the waltz was longer, might just go on and on; then movements out of the corner of his eye. Someone moving through the door, pushing through the crowd of dancers to old man Rowland's table. Old man Rowland staring as the man spoke, getting heavily to his feet, walking to the band platform, slowly raising his hand. The music stopped.

All around the room, dancers twirled to a halt, eyes caught by the pale face of the man in the clean white suit that was just beginning to be wrinkled around the knees and elbows. What does he want now, the old bastard? Nicu was thinking. He's had his say. He looked at Margaret, wanting to laugh with her at old man Rowland. Rowland waiting, his face serious; like someone has died, Nicu thought.

"My friends," Rowland began slowly, "I came before you earlier tonight to speak of an historic occasion." There was no sound in the room but held-in breathing. "Little did I know, that before the evening was well begun, I would have to tell you of a far different, far graver, historic event." He stopped again, and everyone seemed to draw breath together. What is this, what trick is this? Nicu was thinking. What was there anywhere in the world for old man Rowland to get upset about? "The news has just reached the telegraph office that our dear Mother Country, our beloved England," again he stopped, as if overcome by his feelings, "has declared war on Germany." There were shocked looks; a few men cheered. What does it mean? Nicu wondered. Mother England—what was that? Mother England at war with Germany. England, not Canada. It had nothing to do with him.

"... not a war of our seeking. I'm sure you all know how hard England has worked to keep the peace in Europe—none laboured more diligently to try to confine... " He didn't understand, couldn't think; the room was too warm, everyone afraid to breathe; laboured diligently, what was that? "... not possible. The Kaiser has answered our plea for peace by trampling on the neutrality and integrity of a peaceful country." He remembered something about this; a newspaper from Regina, asking the Germans to stay out of Belgium, but that was so far away; Margaret looked at him, fear in her eyes, knowing something he didn't know. "... rush to the defence of our ravished ally." Cheers rose in the room, waves of cheers that seemed to roll over him, making it hard to breathe; Margaret's eyes were fixed again on Rowland.

"What this means for Canada," there was a sudden silence in the room, "I don't need to tell you. It goes without saying," his voice grew louder, deeper, his breathing faster, "that Canada will come to the aid of the Mother—Canada, I say, will be ready, and—" his voice was drowned by the rushing waves of cheers. Rowland looked at the people, tears in his eyes. People cheering, grabbing each other's arms, dancing in place like hot fat in a frying pan. Again the white arms went up. Margaret's hand tightened around his.

"I know the town of Coteau will not be among the last of Britain's supporters and protectors in her time of need, but will rise to the defence loyally and courageously. I *know* our young men will be ready," he was almost shouting. There it was, Nicu thought, there it was: the young men; they want the young men. "I *know* they will not wait to be asked." The cheers were deafening, echoed slowly through the room, like waves moving through water, as Rowland bowed his head, then stepped down, walking through the crowd to his table. Margaret's eyes met Nicu's; now they both understood.

The mayor made for the platform, wanting to speak too, but the crowd wasn't looking, everyone talking at once. He spoke to the band, and a roll of drums and a low chord on the piano brought them to silence. "Ladies and Gentlemen," said Lazbee, "the King." And the band was playing the familiar song, the people fusing to stiff attention, the Dominescus watching in wonder and copying the movements, as the first voices began the anthem. Margaret and Nicu looking at each other, uncertain, then singing too, as they did every morning when they went to school together. He felt foolish, singing a children's song; he didn't feel what these others felt; didn't want to go to any war; didn't believe they wanted to go to any war either. The piano player, hitting the chords hard that ended the song; then cheering, wild, with a new sound in it, as if some restraining hold was broken. Another song beginning, the people singing even louder, but he didn't know this one: "Rule Britannia, Britannia rule the waves," they sang, and he and Margaret just stared at each other, hands still locked, as if they had grown together. Again the song ended in fierce cheering, and a voice yelled from the back of the room: "A drink! A drink!" and "Let's have a toast to old England!" The shout was taken up around the room, and Arthur Rowland nodded to his son, who rose and spoke to the bartender, and in a moment it was done; the bar was open and the drinks were on old man Rowland. Men swarmed around the bar, emptying glasses as fast as Ralph could fill them. Then ignoring him, they grabbed bottles and filled their own glasses. Then the Rowlands got up, almost unnoticed, walked through the billiard room, and left by the hotel lobby.

Nicu felt Margaret's hand tighten; her brother James had come up and was standing beside her. "Father wants you," he said, and with his stocky body and suspicious eyes, he was a younger model of his father. Margaret looked at Nicu, unsure what to do, and the noise in the room seemed to fill his mind. "Father wants you," he said again, more loudly, and took her free arm. Nicu started to raise his arm to stop him, but Margaret looked at him: no, her look pleaded, don't. She pulled her hand free and went with her brother.

The band was playing again, people singing over the noise around the bar, swaying to the music as if blown by the wind. Men at the bar pushed and grabbed, and it seemed that in the few minutes that had passed they had become completely drunk. Nicu watched them milling around the bar, their excited faces reflected in the mirror, bloated and distorted in the flickering candlelight. Near the door men passed around their own bottles, laughing and cheering. Some moved into the street, shouting and singing. Someone pushed roughly against his shoulder. "We'll fix those filthy Germans," a voice said behind him. There was a crash of china as the big cake was knocked, almost unnoticed, to the floor, its candied buildings squashed to shapeless lumps. Doctor Bentley stood staring at it, a bewildered old man now with tears streaming down his face.

Nicu looked around the room for someone not part of the mad frenzy. Israel and his wife had gathered up their children, who'd been sleeping along with the other children in the billiard room, and they were leaving the dance. Alan, still standing at the back of the room, abruptly turned and left. There was a flurry of movement at the bar as a flashing elbow knocked over three of the candles, and Ralph the bartender lunged to catch them before they burned the polished wood.

Nicu looked at mama and tata. He could see they felt out of place here now and wanted to leave. Mama was heading for the billiard room to get Gheorghe. Nicu wanted to be gone too, but he couldn't go without speaking to Margaret. He saw her with her parents at the side of the room. He hesitated, then walked towards them, but he was too late. Her parents were leading her away through the billiard room.

"Excuse me," someone had taken his arm, "are you Nick Dominescu?" It was a young man he'd seen around town, with blue eyes and short curly hair, a friend of the Chisholm boys. He looked excited, and he seemed to be trying not to laugh.

"Yes," he said, "I am Nicu."

"Well, then, someone wants you outside.

Could you just step out for a moment?" And he turned as if to lead Nicu outside.

"Wait, what do you mean? Who wants me?" But the young man wasn't listening to him, and without thinking, Nicu turned and followed him out the door.

Chapter
TWENTY - FOUR

When Nicu didn't come back, Luba and Paia went outside to look for him. Coming around the corner of the hotel, they nearly fell across his legs in the dark grass. Luba reached down to touch his face, felt the congealing blood, the skin warm to the touch. She couldn't see in the dark whether he was breathing, but she held her hand to his lips, feeling after a long moment the warmth of his breath. She nodded at Paia, and without a word he ran to get Sofie and Stefan. She heard his feet on the gravel path, then many steps, people running.

She heard someone moaning. Sofie, kneeling in the grass, hands stretched out to touch Nicu's face. "He is alive, mama," Luba said, and Sofie turned on her with wild eyes, angry that Luba had dared to speak of the thing she feared most. Then Stefan was handing the sleeping Gheorghe to Luba, sending Paia to fetch Chan from his store. Bending, he was touching Nicu, trying to find out what was wrong.

In a few minutes Paia was back with Chan, his gaunt body dressed only in trousers and boots over his long underwear. He carried a small basin of water and had a towel over his arm. When he saw Nicu, the tears ran down his cheeks, as if it were his own son, and he couldn't speak for a moment. Then he said, "You must have the doctor."

"No!" cried Sofie. "We can't do that."

"You must," Chan said. "He may be hurt bad."

They knew where the doctor was. At the dance, standing back against a side wall, watching the madness, one of the few who didn't join in the singing and drinking.

"No," Sofie said. "Please, no." She looked at Chan and Stefan, then down at Nicu, still unconscious. Finally she whispered, "All right. Go then."

In a few minutes, Chan was back with old Dr. Bentley. He looked surprised when he saw who was hurt, but he didn't say anything, just bent down to look at Nicu. He examined the cuts on his face, then checked for broken bones.

"There don't seem to be any broken bones," he said. He took the towel and basin of water Chan had provided and began cleaning a cut over Nicu's eye. Then he reached into a pocket inside his jacket and pulled out a small case of medical instruments. He got out a needle and catgut thread and prepared to sew up the cut.

A tiny cry escaped Sofie. Luba gave Gheorghe to Paia and went and held her mother. She felt Sofie's body, rigid with fear, wanting to stop the doctor before he could harm Nicu, but unable to speak. Luba held her tightly, as Sofie turned away, unable to watch as the doctor deftly sewed up the cut. Luba stroked her hair. "It's done, mama," she said when the doctor had finished.

The doctor reached into another inner pocket and brought out a silver flask. Gently he raised Nicu's head and watched for some sign of consciousness. Nicu opened his eyes for a moment and moaned. "Here," the doctor said, "drink some of this."

"What is it?" Sofie cried.

"Just some whiskey," he said. "It will help with the pain, if nothing else." And he held Nicu's head while he drank a little of the whiskey. Then he lowered Nicu's head back to the grass.

"I think your son will be all right," he said. "His head is injured, a concussion, I think, but I hope there will be no permanent harm. Perhaps if you could take him to Mr. Chan's for the night, I could look in on him tomorrow. Just keep him quiet in bed for a few days, and he should mend right enough."

Dr. Bentley rose to leave. Stefan took money

from his purse and offered it to him.

"There's nothing to pay," the doctor said. "I hope your boy will feel better soon." Stefan hesitated, still holding out the money. "You'd better go home soon," Bentley said. "They've all gone crazy in there." Before Stefan could say anything, the doctor was moving away down the dark street. "Good night," he said, and he was gone.

Sofie began to cry in Luba's arms. The doctor had touched her boy. She had let him. He might have hurt Nicu's eyes, the needle was so close. She remembered the day when the doctors said they must take Trian's tonsils. All this time, she had not forgiven Stefan for saying yes. And now she, Sofie, had also said yes.

"We must take him home tonight," she said.

"But Sofie, maybe it would be better to take him to Chan's place," Stefan said.

"No!" she cried. "He must come home with us."

So Paia went for the wagon and drove it near to where Nicu lay. Then they carried him gently to the wagon, and settled him down on the blankets, covering him against the cool night. They lay Gheorghe down beside him, and Luba and Paia sat in the back with them. Sofie and Stefan sat on the front seat. Just as they were about to drive off, Nicu suddenly sat up.

"Where's Margaret?" he cried, his eyes wild

and unfocused.

"She's coming along later," Luba said, hoping he would believe her.

"Oh, that's good," Nicu said, relieved. "She is eighteen years old now." Then he lay back and fell asleep at once.

Finally they drove away, waving to Chan, who still stood in the street holding the basin of water. As they moved beyond the lighted houses of the town, they became aware of the cool night air, crisp with the first hint of fall. Sofie and Luba wrapped their shawls tighter around their shoulders, and Gheorghe nestled down under his blanket. As the road took them into the country, no one spoke. They just wanted to get home, and to sleep, and to forget this night.

Although Stefan drove slowly so the wagon wouldn't jolt, Luba found that her back and legs were getting stiff. Today she felt so heavy, and the whole centre of her weight seemed to have shifted to her belly, where her baby was growing. She tried not to listen to Nicu breathing heavily through his mouth. She put out her hand and smoothed his hair, but he never stirred.

She thought of the doctor bending over Nicu, saw his hands moving over Nicu's face, his arms, his legs. And she thought, maybe it wasn't his fault when Trian died. Maybe it was an accident, and they didn't mean to hurt him. She wondered if mama and tata were thinking the

same thing. As the wagon moved slowly down
the road, she became convinced that it was true,
and she was glad.

She became aware of traces of white in the
sky, like patches of cloud reflecting the moon.
They began to move, thinning and lengthening
out so that a big round patch became a long
twisting shape that curved and flowed as they
watched. One part of it would disappear, and a
new shape would grow in another part of the sky.
At first these shapes moved only in the north, but
as they stretched and grew, they moved directly
overhead and quickly expanded to fill the sky.

Now the shapes were no longer silvery white
only, but red, violet, green. The waving shapes
swelled in the sky, seemed to loom close to the
earth, sending down filaments of moving fire,
until it seemed to be all around them. Stefan let
the horses come to a stop as they all watched.
Kosma had told them what people called these
lights in the sky. The Northern Lights. No one
knows what makes it, he'd said. They had seen
the dancing shapes many times before, but never
like this, as though the sky was on fire, dipping so
close that once Luba put her hand to her face, almost certain she'd been touched.

She was surprised to find that she wasn't
afraid. The shifting light seemed to flow through
her, bringing her strength. She thought of the
baby growing inside her, touched by the dancing

lights. Her baby would be fearless and strong. She opened her body to the swaying lights.

Chapter
TWENTY-FIVE

Nicu waited. His head ached, and he could feel the pull of the tight stitches in the cut over his eye. It had taken him a long time to walk to the coulee. He'd had to sneak away when mama wasn't watching. He looked around him. The poplars were shorter, scrubbier, than he remembered. Looking at them now, it seemed impossible they could have sheltered a herd of wild horses. And yet they had been here. He had seen them. The grass was as he remembered: dry and wiry, cured by the sun to a pale buff; thickest in the coulee, around the trees. The heat of the late afternoon sun on his bruised face made Nicu want to enter the trees.

He walked into the trees. For a moment he felt sick to his stomach, and he reached out and grabbed a tree trunk to steady himself. The bark felt smooth and faintly warm. The smallest trees were no thicker than his wrist; the biggest, half a foot thick. Two cold nights this last week, and already the leaves were turning, fluttering green-gold flames in the waning light. He was deep in the trees now, so hidden by leaves that anyone looking down from the hills would be unable to see him. It was cooler among the trees, and they gave him a pleasant feeling of safety. Deer had sheltered here too, their hard brown droppings scattered along a path that wound through the bluff. He passed a tree with a magpie's nest, a tangled mass of twigs, but there was no sign of birds.

He came to a small clearing. On the ground he saw the remains of an old fire: a circle of blackened rocks, decaying bits of burnt wood. Not old enough to be from the Indians, but an old fire. Maybe someone had camped here: a hunter in the fall, or a Metis from Willow Bunch, riding out in spring to take part in a round-up or work on a sheep-shearing gang. Lachance said this place was on the old freighting route to Wood Mountain. He'd showed Nicu the faint trail through the coulees. When his family had come to Canada they'd thought of it as a vast and empty land. But Lachance said his people had been here for hundreds of years. And before that, the Indians had been here even longer. Nicu had seen their stone tent rings, but they never seemed to come here any more, at least no one had seen them. But he knew now that the land had not been empty. At the dance a man had called him a dirty foreigner. But Alan had said once: "We are all foreigners here." Nicu saw the land, the sky, differently now. Never again would he look out and see an empty land.

He remembered the horses, running free across the hills. Yes, he thought, they were real. They were here. He sat down on the cool earth of the clearing, and he grieved for the earth-coloured horse. And he grieved for himself because the men had beaten him, and because they had hurt him more deeply than the bruises and ache of his body. He cried for the stallion and for himself, and for Lachance, who was like a brother, and who would not ride again.

Nicu had decided one thing. He would not go to the war. He didn't know where England was, or Belgium, or Germany, and he didn't want to find out. He had come all the way to Canada with his family, crossed a gale-ridden sea from the old country, and they were none of them, ever, going back. He didn't want to go back, and he didn't want to kill anyone, not even the Rowlands.

He saw a tree with dark markings in the bark: letters enclosed in a circle. He came close to see them: N.D. + M.C., Nicu Dominescu and Margaret Chisholm. He must have carved them, but he couldn't remember doing it. He examined the tree, looking for traces of his own way of forming letters. He thought they looked familiar, and tried again to remember coming here. Could he forget such a thing? He noticed another tree with letters in a circle, about three feet away. L.D. + P.M., Luba Dominescu and Paia Manescu. So that was it. Luba had carved these letters. He wondered how long she had known about him and Margaret. He thought of her walking away from the house, coming to the trees. He couldn't imagine her bringing a knife. And the fire? Had she made the fire too? He tried to imagine these things, but it was hard, and he thought, I didn't know you.

He rolled down the sleeves of his flannel shirt. The sun had gone behind the hills, and it was getting cool. He would go sit on the side of the hill, facing south, to wait for Margaret. They had arranged it all weeks ago. By sundown she would come to the poplar bluff in the coulee. They would plan their wedding.

As he left the trees and walked up the hill, the air was warmer again. He climbed the grassy hill almost to the top, climbed back into slanting light, sat down on a wide flat rock. Once again the sun was hot against his skin, but his mind seemed to remain below in the cool dark trees, thinking of secrets, of blackened letters cut into living bark.

He tried not to think about her coming. But the images leapt into his mind. She might walk quietly through the coulee, arriving almost before he could spot her. Or she might run over the top of the hill and shout to him, and he would run and circle her in his arms. Perhaps then they would sink to the grass holding each other. Perhaps they would make themselves into a ball and go rolling down the long slope, round and round, like children, till their heads were spinning.

Again the hills cut off the sun, and again he began to feel cool. His mind tried to return to the scenes of the dance, but he wouldn't think of it. He forced his mind to think of trees; himself among trees, shaded by leaves, surrounded by the slender trunks, warm smooth bark, uneven curving letters burning themselves into his mind. He held the scene as he watched the coulee darken, light in the sky fading slowly, until in the west he saw the first star; until all the sun's light faded, leaving the prairie still bright under the cold light of the moon, his body chilled, aching. Margaret wasn't coming.

Chapter
TWENTY-SIX

It was the first time he had been late for work; not very late, but he knew by the sun that he was not quite on time. He had ridden to town from home this morning, his mind full of questions; seeing her house from the road, wanting to go there and take her away. All the way to town, wanting to go there and take her away. All the way to town, wanting to turn back.

It must be about eight-thirty, and already the sun was fiercely hot. He wore a light straw hat, but even so, he was sweating. It was his turn to load the kiln. Jesus! Lanks would be mad because he was late. Lanks. It seemed like all last week Lanks had had it in for him, he couldn't do anything to suit him; and now with his bruised eye and swollen lip, Lanks would be on his back all day, would harass him through a week of the heaviest jobs. Thank God he could still work. But Margaret had not come.

He forced himself to leave these thoughts, to

try to think of going in to the yard and working. He looked around the yard, now only about a hundred yards away, and realized that nowhere could he see anyone at work. A group of men stood around the gate. He could make out Alan's tall bony frame, gesturing with his arm, and a group of men around him. Alan was talking to Lanks, was yelling at him. Nicu let his horse slow to a walk. What did it mean, men standing around, everyone trying to talk at once? Were they arguing about the steam shovel Rowland wanted to buy? About Alan trying to get the union started? He saw Lanks turn and try to walk away, but Alan grabbed his arm and wouldn't let him by. Lanks's body stiffened, and he shook Alan's hand off his arm, glaring at him, speaking too low for Nicu to hear. He was close now, about thirty yards away, but no one had noticed him. "Listen, Lanks, you bastard—" Alan was shouting.

"No, you listen to me." Lanks was yelling now. "Just get your ass out of here right now, because I don't have to listen to this! Do you hear me?" Nicu saw Alan's arm move to swing at Lanks, and then Israel was there, speaking to him, and his arm slowly dropped to his side. "Jesus!" he said, and walked out the gate, followed by Israel and more slowly by Randy. Nobody spoke, Randy staring straight ahead, looking as though the power of speech had left him.

Nicu got down from the bay horse to wait for them. In the yard, the rest of the men silently watched.

They faced him on the road. "We're fired," Alan said. "All of us." His mouth made a grim line, his eyes angry and narrow. The sun beat down on their heads.

"Fired!" Nicu said. "But why? What did you do?"

Alan looked at him hard, and Israel's eyes had that pitying look. "I said all of us," Alan said.

There it was. He was fired too. "They buy this steam shovel already?" he asked.

"It's got nothin to do with any steam shovel. Lanks just up and fired us." Randy was almost in tears.

"But how he can do that? Can't we go to old man Rowland?" Nicu asked.

"It was Mr. Rowland's orders," Israel said gently.

"It is because we have the man to talk to us about union?" Nicu asked.

"It's because of the union all right," Alan said, "and because he wants to make us join up."

"Join up?" Nicu asked. "What is that?"

"Join the army. Sign up. Volunteer. His kid William's goin to fight the war, and he wants to make damn sure some of us go with him. After all, he said the men of Coteau wouldn't wait to be asked. So he's tellin us."

"Are the other men fired too?" Nicu glanced at the yard, saw men slowly walking back to their places.

Alan shook his head. "So far it's just us."

"So it has to be because of the union," Israel said.

"But I didn't even want no goddamn union." The words were torn from Randy. "What'm I gonna do? What'm I gonna tell my wife?"

"I'm sorry, Randy." Alan looked very tired.

"You're sorry! *Sorry*, for Christ sake! What'm I gonna *do*?" he was almost crying. Nobody said anything. Randy had asked the question Nicu wanted to ask.

"I don't know," Alan said.

"Well, *think* of something! I've got three kids to look after, and another one in the oven!" Randy looked ashamed of his words, but he couldn't stop. "Four kids, goddammit! What'm I gonna do?"

Alan turned away. "Randy, it's not my fault. We had a right to start a union. We had a *right*."

"Oh — shit!" Randy screamed, "what good's a *right* to me? I ain't got a job!" He slammed his fist into his hand.

"Maybe there is work down at Estevan, in the coal fields," Israel said. "I think they will keep on needing coal in wartime, it's not like bricks. Maybe there will be work there."

"But I got a little place here. We put a lot of

work into it, me and Lynnie." Randy's eyes filled with tears. "You think I'd be able to get anything for it now? And how do you know there'll be work? They're probably laying them off down there too. Looks like the only thing a guy can do is enlist. At least you know it's steady—and you sure as hell aren't gonna get your wife in trouble."

"Don't be a fool, Stokes, that's the one thing you *know* you shouldn't do." Alan spoke harshly.

"Yeah, well tell me what to do then, smart guy. Your last plan didn't work out so good."

"For Christ's sake, Randy, let up, will ya? I've got a kid too. You think I wanted to get fired?"

"Listen, all of you," Israel said, "come to my place. We have some coffee, talk about this."

"Oh, the hell with it, I'm goin' home," Randy said. He pointed at Nicu. "It's all his fault. These foreign bastards come and take our jobs—"

"It is not Nick's fault," Israel said.

"Let the foreign bastards go back where they come from. All they do is cause trouble!"

Alan put his hand on Randy's arm. But Randy jerked his arm free, and Alan let his hand drop. Randy glared at him, fists clenched.

"Alan," Israel said, "let him go now." Randy turned and left the road, cutting across a field towards his house on the northwest side of town. They watched him, but he didn't look back. Nicu dismounted and walked beside his two friends, leading the bay mare. He tried to understand what had happened. I've lost my job, he told himself. It can't be. I've lost my job, and Margaret never came.

Chapter
TWENTY - SEVEN

The darkest time of night and the horses running, running. Under his bare thighs the smooth gallop of the earth-coloured horse, its hair rough against his skin. Mares so close around them he feels their warmth. The sound of their running echoes in his ears, and the soft rush of cold wind. Mares, their eyes round and smooth, staring straight ahead as they run. The stallion's body warm against him, and this time he is with the stallion. Against the dark sky, he sees at the front of the herd a smokey grey colt made for running. The stallion snorting and around him the harsh breathing of the horses. Pressing his face into the stallion's warm neck, smelling the sharp sweat, feeling it enter his body until he smells like horses, is one with horses. An explosion shakes the ground, the smokey colt rears. Another roar and it cartwheels gracefully in front of him, falls heavily to ground. The stallion screams. Men are shooting at the stallion, shooting at him. He

*presses his face into the warm neck, his hands
clutch the wiry mane. He feels something terribly cold, like wind rushing through him, and he
knows the bullet has passed through his body and
into the horse. He sees blood in front of his eyes, is
falling, falling.*

He sat straight up in bed, sweat pouring off
him, his body cold as ice. Somewhere very near a
horse whinnied. He jumped up and ran to the
window. Leaves rustled in the poplars around
the garden. In the light of a harvest moon, he
saw a dark figure slide down from a pale horse
and walk to the house. The breeze from the
window was cold against his naked skin. He
heard the porch door open. He ran out of the
room and down the stairs. The kitchen was filled
with moonlight, the floor cold against his feet.
Through the window he could see the stars. He
flung open the kitchen door.

She stepped from the shadowed porch into the
kitchen. The moonlight touched her face, her
clothes, he could see her calm eyes fixed on his
face, and she was reaching out. He put his arms
out to her and she came to him, her arms around
his neck, her face warm against his naked chest,
her hair cool from the touch of wind. He felt her
woolen cloak and the heavy man's trousers rough
against his skin. He held her tight against him,
kissed her hair, her forehead. Her clear dark eyes
looked into his, and he couldn't feel the cold.

Margaret had come, had come.

They sat at the round table with Stefan, the coal oil lamp turned down low. Sofie was in the kitchen, she had the fire going and she was making coffee. She looked confused, all of her fears were coming to pass. Nicu would marry the pale girl, the English girl, the Chisholm girl. His children would be pale and bloodless — like skim milk or white bread. But Stefan had said what was good and kind, what Nicu had known he would say. He would be happy to have Margaret for his daughter.

Sofie brought coffee and they all sat round the table. The wind made a lonely sound like the howling blizzards of winter. In the faint light before the dawn, they heard hoofbeats, distant, but growing louder. Men riding hard. Margaret took Nicu's hand, held it in both of hers. Galloping horses, closer and closer. Then slowing to a walk, snorting and whinnying in the morning cold. Sound of voices, men's voices. Someone knocked loudly on the outside door, kicked at the door with heavy boots.

"Come on out, Dominescu." It was Chisholm's voice. "Get out here, or we're coming in."

"Get Paia," Stefan said to Sofie.

More blows and other voices. Now James Chisholm yelling, his voice harsh as metal scraping against stone. "Come on out, you bastards.

Come on out and fight." They pounded and kicked the door.

"Wait here," Stefan said to Nicu, "I will speak to them."

He walked through the kitchen, opened the door to the dark porch, then the outer door. He stepped outside, under the fading stars. Wind blew hard in his face. In front of their three big sorrels, old man Chisholm stood flanked by his sons, James with a rifle waving in his hand, and John just behind them, a hand on the bridle of Margaret's palomino.

"Where is he?" James asked. "Where is the thieving bastard?" His eyes were dark wells of hatred in his blunt face.

"Where's your boy?" Chisholm demanded, flinty eyes narrowed, stubby legs planted wide.

"My son is inside."

James waved his rifle in Stefan's face. "Get him out here, I'm going to teach him a lesson about stealing." James leaned closer, and Stefan could smell his acrid breath.

"What stealing?"

"He's stolen my horse, and he's stolen my daughter. I want back what's mine."

"My son stole nothing."

"My horse is here, and my daughter's gone," Chisholm said sharply. He stepped forward, ready to spring at Stefan. James, too, seemed to crouch, waiting for some signal. John still held the palomino. He looked hesitant, but he would move if his father ordered it.

"Maybe your daughter ride away on your horse," Stefan suggested.

"Aye, but she's with your son."

"If she is with my son, it is because she want to be with him."

"She has no choice," Chisholm spoke louder, losing control. "I've promised her to Mr. Lazbee, and it's Mr. Lazbee she'll marry."

"She say she will marry my son."

James moved forward, holding the rifle in front of him with both hands. "They're inside, let's go in and get them."

Stefan was afraid. But he thought of his boy buried on the hill, lost because he hadn't known what to say to the doctors. He barred the way. "You can't come in."

"Like hell, we can't. We own the place." James pushed with the gun against Stefan's arm.

Something moved in the porch behind Stefan, then three men stood in front of the porch — Stefan, Paia and Nicu — balancing the strength of the three stone men. "You can't come in here, Chisholm," Stefan said. "Your daughter want to marry my son. She is going to have baby. You think I give my grandchild to Lazbee?"

James shifted the rifle in his hand. Stefan held on to the barrel. "Put your gun down. When you hurt my boy, you are many against one. We see how strong you are when you fight even."

James threw the rifle down. Chisholms moved closer together, like a wall, James with his shoulders tight against the old man's, John keeping a little distance. The three by the porch moved sideways, not to be caught against the house, their arms tense, half bent.

High on the hill a man's scream echoed, a long drawn-out scream of pain and hatred, of mingled joy and fear, lonely as a coyote's howl but overlaid with human grief. He ran raggedly up the hill, nearly falling against the heavy boulders, his hands thrown wide against the sky. At the top he stopped and turned. "Bastards!" he was yelling. "You bastards! I showed you goddamn foreign bastards! You bastards, bastards!"

A horse screamed, hooves pounded against wood, and they no longer watched the man on the hill. They saw the weathered old barn, bursting like dawn into rosy flame, as fire flared in the loft, with its dry hay and the last of the spring's fleece.

"Bring your horses!" Chisholm yelled to his sons. "A fireguard!" They mounted and raced the short slope to the barn. Nicu and Paia ran, with Stefan just behind.

Paia and Nicu stopped at the horse trough. Paia grabbed pails and began to fill them, but Nicu jumped right in the trough, the cold brackish water soaking his clothes, skin, hair. Then he ran for the barn, Paia chasing after him. "No," Paia yelled, "you can't." Thick smoke poured from the loft, was tossed and scattered into the wind. The air smelled of burnt grass and wool burning in its own grease. Nicu reached for the plank that barred the barn doors. Paia grabbed his arm.

"Don't go in there!"

"I've got to save my horse." Nicu shook off Paia's arm, then kicked the plank free. Both men jumped back as a wall of heat and gases exploded outwards, flinging wide the barn doors. Nicu took a deep breath, held it, forced himself to go in. The horses were screaming. Smoke stung his eyes, but he saw the loft, a mass of flames, and the grey colt tethered just inside the barn door. No way to get to the other horses. Nicu grabbed the colt's halter, but it couldn't move, its body shaking like the day he found it in the ravine. When he pulled at the halter, it reared and kicked, striking his ankle. Tearing off his belt, he smacked its rump and half-led, half-dragged it from the barn. And then he was gasping for breath, his eyes stinging, his throat aching. Paia helped him lead the colt to the corral by the horse trough and tie it to a rail. Nicu stroked its neck and flanks gently, speaking softly. Inside the barn, his bay mare and the faithful old Zaica screamed their deaths. His face felt hot, and when he touched his forehead, the eyebrows came away in a charred powder. His throat hurt and his ankle throbbed, but he had saved the grey colt.

At the trough, Paia worked furiously, and the pump sounded near breaking, rough scream of iron on iron. Sofie and Margaret ran to the barn with pails of water, and Stefan threw them on the fire. Nicu ran to help.

The Chisholms had harnessed their saddle horses to the rusted plough by the barn, James and John steadying them, dodging the stamping feet, and Chisholm hitching them to the singletree. Then the old man drove the makeshift team up the hill where tongues of wind-driven fire snaked across the prairie towards the Chisholm place. Chisholm worked them back and forth, the dull plough catching on stones and slipping from the furrows. His sons wet gunny sacks at the trough and beat at the flames. At the top of the hill, a man laughed, a dark shape against the brightening sky.

Now Stefan pumped and the others carried the buckets of water. Wind blasted the hot smoke into their eyes, bits of soot dropped on their faces and arms. Flaming shingles vaulted across the yard, landing here and there in the dirt, and on the roof, where Luba was stamping out the tiny fires. On the hill, Chisholm now ploughed in a wide half-circle around the barn, cutting off the fire's path.

The barn burned with a soft roar distinct from the roar of the wind. They couldn't hear the animals any more. Timbers flamed brilliantly, outlining the barn against the sky. Then a crackling of rafters, a sighing sound, and the barn collapsed. In the centre of the fire, everything was being consumed.

Now they worked on small piles of burning rubble, the Chisholm sons beating their sacks at the edges of the fire. Chisholm slowed at his ploughing, and Stefan stopped pumping and took Sofie's bucket. In the way a storm dies away, the fire was dying, moving back in on itself. The fireguard was finished. Chisholm was unhitching his horses, turning them back into saddle horses. The man on the hill, sitting now on a wide flat rock, abandoned himself to weeping.

Finally, only a few burning heaps remained, and everyone stopped. Chisholms faced Dominescus. Margaret stood with Dominescus, watching her father with steady eyes. For a moment it seemed as though Chisholm must give his hand to Stefan. But the moment passed and could not be found again.

"Father," Margaret said, "I'm going to marry Nicu."

"Aye," he said, "marry who you please."

The man was coming down the hill, staggering, his hair and clothes covered in dust, as though he'd fallen and wallowed like an animal.

His hair, dirty and straggly, trailed on the smokey wind, plastered in front to his sweaty forehead. He looked like a dirty walking scarecrow, ragged and empty, making his way through the blackened grass. Tears ran down his cheeks, making muddy furrows through the dust. He cried with the abandon of a child, but in a man's voice. He was dead drunk, his body loose as a child's rag doll, chest heaving with sobs. Nicu stared hard at Randy Stokes, acrid air stinging his throat. He thought Randy wanted to tell him something, but he stopped beside the Chisholms.

"I showed them," Randy was telling old man Chisholm. "I showed those foreign bastards." He pulled at James Chisholm's sleeve. "I showed the bastards, didn't I?" His voice pleaded.

"You're stinking drunk, man," James said, jerking his arm free.

"I showed 'em, didn't I?" Randy was asking Chisholm.

"You're a goddamn fool!" Chisholm said, turning away. John Chisholm, too, stepped back. Randy looked around at Stefan, at Paia, at Nicu. He stumbled towards Nicu.

"You spoiled everything. Spoiled everything, you bastard." He lunged, aiming a punch that was wide of Nicu's face, landed in air, put him off balance, and he fell forward on Nicu's chest, one arm around his neck. Nicu steadied Randy, pushed him slowly to his feet.

Chapter
TWENTY-EIGHT

The violin sings and the circle begins to move, too quickly for the dancers to feel the touch of fall in the air. Sweat glistens on their foreheads. The dance that began in the old Sweet Grass schoolhouse has moved outside for the circle dance, the Romanian hora. Around a bonfire in the flat oval in front of the school, the circle moves. Bodies dip and sway, making long waving shadows against the grass. Nicu and Margaret lead the dance, and once again Margaret is wearing the rose-coloured dress.

Whiskey, tsuica, the smell of roasting lamb. In the flickering light, one man leaps high, leaps high, his black eyes gleaming like berries. He wears a flowing peasant shirt and trousers, his arms and legs a blur of movement like the wings of a hummingbird. Smell of sage, smell of sweat, cool air on warm skin, sudden sadness at the waning of the year, of the sun. A tall dark-haired woman sits by herself, because her husband has gone home without her, taking his two flinty sons. But as for herself, she will stay. Near by, on a wooden bench, the other mother sits. She thinks for a moment of the children she has lost and the boy who died at sea. Then she watches her oldest son dancing, and wraps herself more tightly in a wonderful shawl embroidered with birds and flowers. She remembers the hummingbird, its tiny wings whirling, in the bush by the window, in a country far away.

One by one the men from the brick yard dance Margaret around the circle. The yard is closed now. Most of these men are signing up, going to fight the war. Going to war with young William Rowland. Randy is already gone, into the infantry. But Alan will stay. Israel will stay. And Nicu will stay. He is going with Margaret to work on a ranch in the Cypress Hills. He has heard that it is beautiful country there, beautiful as the old country. Like his father, he will trust to his skills with animals. Perhaps one day the smoke-grey colt will sire a herd of beautiful horses.

On the steps of the school, a tall Chinese man sits next to a tall slender boy. One hand holds a cup of strong tea, the other rests lightly on the boy's shoulders. Beside them a small black-haired woman sits, her hands folded neatly on her knees, watching the dancing.

Beneath them, on the very bottom step, a

woman with hair the colour of wheat stubble holds a tiny baby in her arms. The baby has gleaming black eyes, like berries. She hands the baby to the Chinese woman and goes to dance with her husband. The dance goes round. Hands part for a moment to make a place for a dark-eyed young man and a young woman in a creamy muslin blouse who is going to have a child, and who has decided not to be afraid. The dance goes round and round.

For a moment everything seems safe. Tonight no one will go home. There is food, music, fire against the darkness. There is grass and the cool stars.

The music begins again. The man with the flute is smiling, but he seems to be looking at something far away. The burly man playing the fiddle steps with his new boots in a fresh cowpie and laughs till the tears stream down his cheeks. A dog barking at a prairie chicken falls into a slough, shakes the wetness out of its coat, and for once no one chases it away. People eat fat strips of meat and throw some of the fat to the dogs. Far away a coyote sings.

The bride has ribbons in her hair, crimson ribbons.

Everyone knows the bride is pregnant.

The shouts of the dancing men echo through the hills.

No one will go home tonight.

The night gets cooler.
They build up the fire.
No one goes home.
And then the sun.

GLOSSARY OF
Romanian Words

tata	father
Maica Domnolui	mother of God
asha	so, thus; often used as an exclamation of surprise
draguts (m)	dear one
dragutsa (f)	
draga (f)	
buna ziua	good day
boyar	member of aristocratic land-owning class
tsuica	Romanian plum brandy
doamne	mild exclamation, similar to *my goodness*
sarmale	cabbage rolls
mamaliga	cornmeal mush
me tu!	hey you!
buna dimineatsa	good morning
dumnezeu	God
baba	old woman
bun amic	good friend
musca	fly
multsam	thank you
fantoma	ghost
babushka	old woman
somnoros	sleepy one
bashîna	fart

zmeu	devil
pishoarca	pissabed
momaie	scarecrow
esta	isn't it?
cacat	shit
copil de tsatsa	child at the breast
maicutsa	mother
colibri	hummingbird
placinta	Romanian pastry, like very thin strudel
pentru numele lui dumnezeu	in the name of God
me tu drac	hey, you devil
fiu mia	my son
zamfir	sapphire

BARBARA SAPERGIA

Barbara Sapergia is an accomplished writer of plays, poetry, radio dramas and fiction. Her first collection of poetry, *Dirt Hills Mirage*, appeared in 1980. Her poems and short stories have appeared in numerous journals and anthologies, including the Coteau Books' collections, *Number One Northern* (1977), *Sundogs* (1980), *Saskatchewan Gold* (1982), *100% Cracked Wheat* (1983), *Prairie Jungle* (1985) and *Sky High* (1988).

Additionally, Barbara has written many plays over the years, seven of which have been produced since 1982. These include "Lokkinen" (published by Playwrights Canada, 1984), "The Willow Bunch Giant" (with Geoffrey Ursell), "Matty & Rose," "The Great Orlando" and "Roundup," plus two plays for children, "The Skipping Show" and "Blizzard and the Christmas Spirit" (with Geoffrey Ursell).

More recently, several of Barbara's plays and radio dramas have aired on CBC Radio Saskatchewan, "Grandma's Foot," "The Giant Who Wept" (with Geoffrey Ursell), "Old Crocks," "Double Talk," and "Roundup." "Playing the Game" a dramatic look at living on welfare aired on CBC Radio's "Morningside" in 1988. CBC TV has produced two of Barbara's film scripts, "Any Farmers Left" and "Midnight in Moose Jaw" (with Ron Coneybeare and Geoffrey Ursell).

Foreigners is Barbara's first novel and was originally published in 1984. In this novel, as in some of her other work, Barbara returns to her Romanian roots and a rural Saskatchewan setting. Her work displays a versatile range from the light and humourous to the more serious and thought-provoking.

Barbara was born and grew up in Moose Jaw, Saskatchewan. She studied at the University of Saskatchewan and the University of Manitoba, receiving a Masters degree in English literature. She has taught English at the University of Victoria and the University of British Columbia. Barbara is a founding member of the Thunder Creek Publishing Co-operative.

Currently Barbara is a full-time writer and resides in Saskatoon, Saskatchewan with her husband, writer Geoffrey Ursell.

MORE TITLES FROM COTEAU BOOKS

Look for other Coteau Books at your favorite bookstore. For a complete catalogue of publications—fiction, poetry, drama, criticism, non-fiction and children's literature—please write to 401–2206 Dewdney Avenue, Regina, Saskatchewan S4R 1H3.